THE BEST EROTIC SHORT STORIES OF 2022

EXPLICIT ADULT EROTICA FEATURING FIRST TIMES, THREESOMES, ROUGH SEX, ANAL SEX, ROLE-PLAY, GANG BANGS, LESBIAN SEX, CUCKOLD, OLDER-YOUNGER, MFM, TABOO, AND MORE...

EDITED BY

RAYNA RUSSELL

GO PUBLISHING

CONTENTS

CHAPTER 1

BURNING UP

BY SHAR SILVER

"This is ridiculous." I rolled my eyes, snatched the remote off the coffee table, and switched off the TV. Then I ran my fingers through my hair and stretched my legs out ahead of me. "I can't believe all the hype surrounding this movie."

Drew brought his arms over his head, and his chest rode up, revealing perfectly chiseled abs and a defined trail of hair that disappeared under the waistband of his shorts. "You're telling me that you aren't curious?"

I looked away and cleared my throat. "I am curious, but I'm not that curious."

"So, you wouldn't ever want to try something like that?"

I raised an eyebrow and twisted my head to look at him. "Are you being serious right now?"

Drew sat up straighter and smirked. "Of course, I'm being serious. It's hot shit."

I tilted my head sideways, and my eyes roamed over his face, stopping at his dark brown eyes. "So, you're really into that stuff?"

Drew shrugged. "Yeah, I am, but it's not a big deal if you don't want to try it out."

"It's so degrading."

"It's not like that at all," Drew maintained before reaching for both of my hands. "That's an inaccurate representation. BDSM is as much about mutual trust as it is about pleasure."

I glanced down at our hands, then back up at his face. "So, when you made that bet when we were playing Go fish, that wasn't an accident, was it?"

Drew shook his head. "I wanted to see your reaction."

"Okay."

"That's it?"

I shook my head. "No, I'm just not sure how I feel about it."

"Does me telling you it's not degrading help?"

I paused. "It does."

Drew brought my hands up to his lips, his hot breathing sending my insides into a frenzy. "We don't have to if you don't want to, Kayla. You know that I'm never going to force you to do anything you don't feel comfortable with."

I nodded. "I know."

The two of us had been dating for a year, but we'd been friends for a lot longer, and if there was one thing I knew without a shadow of a doubt, it was that Drew would never hurt me. And given the active and exciting sex life he'd maintained before meeting me, I was only surprised it had taken him this long to open up.

I'd had my suspicions for a while now.

Drew wasn't exactly the vanilla type, and I'd known he was holding back, but it was another thing entirely to realize that he was the spanking and bondage type. Watching the movie with him made it apparent, but while I was intrigued, I wasn't sure if it was enough to get me to agree.

Not right away, at least.

Drew shifted closer, released my hands, and threw an arm over my shoulder. "So, what do you think?"

I stared at him. "You actually want to try this with me?"

Drew chuckled and pressed a kiss to the side of my head. "Of course, I do, dummy. You're my girlfriend."

"And you're okay with the fact that I haven't done anything like that before?"

"I am more than okay with that. I'll teach you everything you need to know. We'll go as slow or as fast as you want, and we can have a safe word."

I studied his profile underneath soft fluorescent lightning and blew out a breath. "If I was curious, and I'm not saying that I am, how would it go?"

"You'd have to be comfortable first, and of course, we'd have to settle on a safe word," Drew explained, bringing his legs to rest on the coffee table. Out on the street, there was a motor revving, followed by the sound of shrieks and giggles. Then a strong gust of spring wind burst in through the open window, filling the living room with the smell of wildflowers and honeysuckle.

"What else?"

"If there's something you don't want to try at all, you have to let me know ahead of time," Drew continued, his breath warm on the side of my face. His grip around my shoulders tightened, and my stomach dipped. "But it would be a lot of fun. I promise."

"I don't know."

I couldn't deny that a part of me was intrigued, mostly because it was Drew. I wanted to see him let loose and have sex with me with wild and reckless abandon. But, another part of me was worried I would be so bad it would turn him off altogether.

Drew kissed my cheek and pulled back. "It's okay, Kay. It was just a thought, anyway. We don't have to."

I leaned back against the couch and studied his face. "Since it means so much to you, I'm willing to try it out, but I want to pick the stuff we get to use."

Drew's smile was slow and seductive, sending desire straight to my belly. "Deal."

Immediately, he stood up and pulled me up to my feet. He gave me a long and thorough kiss that left my skin tingling before he disappeared into the bedroom. When he returned, he was barefoot and carrying a box. I saw the hunger in his eyes and etched onto his features, and butter-flies erupted in my stomach.

It's Drew. Of course, you're going to enjoy this. You love the shit out of this guy, and it means a lot to him, so why not?

"That didn't take long at all," I teased.

Drew set the box down on the carpeted floor and winked. "I like a woman who knows what she wants."

Slowly, I pushed myself up to my feet and wandered over to the box. Underneath the light of the living room, I bent down and brought my hands to rest on top of my shorts. After a brief examination, I pushed aside an all-black whip and a set of balls. Then, I picked up a pair of furry handcuffs and a black eye mask with hot stuff emblazoned across the front in gold. My lips twitched as I held them up to the light.

"It was the only thing they had when I brought it," Drew muttered, refusing to meet my gaze. "What's your safe word?"

"Eggplants," I replied without preamble.

"Eggplants?"

"I hate eggplants, so it makes sense," I reminded him with a small smile. "And I want to go slow today. We can talk about the other stuff later."

Drew nodded and straightened his back. "You've got it, gorgeous. I promise you, this is going to be so much fun. You'll love it, and if you don't, we can stop right away."

My heart thudded against my chest, and the butterflies in my stomach erupted into a frenzy. Slowly, I rose up to my feet, and a shiver of anticipation raced up and down my spine. Drew took the handcuffs and mask and set them down on the couch. Slowly, he wrapped his arms around me and pulled me to him.

When I tilted my head back to look up at him, I forgot how to breathe. Until he lowered his lips to mine, and my chest swelled with emotion. I released a deep, shaky breath and melted against him, feeling every inch of him pressed against me. Drew's hands traveled up the length of my back and stopped at the back of my neck. He cupped my face in his hands and deepened the kiss.

As soon as we both began to pant, he leaned back and offered me a bright smile.

With that, he took my hand and led me to the bedroom. There, he took his time undressing me before removing his own clothes in two quick movements. When he was done, his mouth found mine, and we fell onto the bed, a tangle of limbs and heavy breathing. Drew pulled back a short while later and grinned at me before he slid off the bed. He returned, carrying the handcuffs in one hand and the blindfold in the other. My heart jumped into my throat as I watched him approach and crawl onto the bed next to me. Before I knew what was happening, Drew had handcuffed me to the headboard with one arm on either side of me and my legs spread open.

"Are they too tight? Do you want me to try something else?"

I gave a quick tug and shook my head. "No, I'm okay. It's actually comfortable."

Drew leaned between in and kissed me. "It's what the fur is for. Do you want me to use the blindfold?"

"Not yet."

Drew sat back on his legs, his eyes roaming over every inch of exposed skin. I tried not to squirm while he studied me, but before long, the heat in my legs grew to be too much. So, I pressed my thighs together, and Drew gave me a wicked smirk in return. He jumped off the bed and flicked on the lamp. Then, he switched off the blinding white lights, casting the room in a warm yellow glow. Slowly, he leaned forward, crawled over the mattress, and pressed hot, open-mouthed kisses to my neck. His tongue darted out to lick a path up to my ears and back down while his hands moved over my feverish skin. My lips parted, and I made a low, squeaking noise. Soon, his fingers were around my breasts, tugging and pinching until both nipples had begun to stiffen.

And I was soaking wet.

Holy shit.

This felt better than anything I'd ever experienced.

And the knowledge that I was tied up and completely at Drew's mercy stirred something within me, a fierce longing I didn't know I had. So, I threw my head back, arched my bag, and didn't mind when the handcuffs dug into my wrists. Drew shifted, so he was looming over me, his erection pressing against the inside of my thighs. I tried to wrap my legs around him, but he pinned them down on either side of his hips.

"You're not allowed to do that," Drew told me in a husky voice. "I'm in charge right now, and you have to do whatever I say."

I pouted. "What about I want?"

"I'm going to give you everything you want." Drew returned to kissing me, his mouth covering one nipple, then the other, until I was panting. "And more. You're going to be begging for more, Kayla. Do you understand?"

I gave a quick nod.

Drew's hand darted between us and moved down, settling over my folds. "I can see that you're already wet."

"Mm-hmm."

"I think I should finger fuck you first." Drew pushed one finger, then another. "I want you to watch me while I do it."

I kept my eyes open and looked down, my pulse quickening when I did. "Shit."

Drew's fingers moved left, then right. "Feels good, doesn't it?"

"It feels amazing."

Drew began to move up and down, his eyes never leaving my face. "Are you sure about that?"

"Yes." I breathed, resisting the urge to squeeze my eyes shut and moan. "Oh, God, Drew. This feels so good."

Drew smirked. "Good, but we're not done yet."

He abruptly removed his hands and brought them up to his mouth. While I watched, he licked his fingers one by one. I made a low noise in the back of my throat and strained against the bindings, but they didn't budge. My stomach tightened as Drew placed one arm on either side of me and positioned himself at my entrance.

I squeezed my eyes shut and waited.

Nothing happened.

As soon as I opened my eyes, Drew slammed into me, filling me to the brim before he withdrew. "I told you that I want you to watch me, Kay. Watch me while I fuck you, okay?"

I moaned in response.

"Good girl. That's it. You're mine." Drew's thrusts were long and measured, easing out of me, then slamming back in again, using more force each and every time. In no time at all, I was covered in sweat and panting, my heart racing against my chest. He moved with a fluidity and ease that had me moaning and writhing, unable to get enough off of him. Yet, each time I tried to edge him closer, he stopped. So, I alternated between scowling and pouting until Drew allowed me to wrap my legs around him, pushing him all the way in.

It felt like I was going to explode into a million pieces.

Abruptly, Drew threw one leg up over his shoulder and eased in further, forcing my muscles to expand and contract.

I focused on his face, studying every inch of him until he began to move again, harder this time.

When I began to chant his name, my nails digging into the inside of my palms, he buried himself and held absolutely still until my orgasm washed over me.

Wave after wave of pain had me writhing and spasming while my vision grew white. By the time I settled, my breathing was erratic, and my entire body tingled. Still, I was in the handcuffs and aware that Drew had pulled out and was now kissing a path down to my pussy. Wordlessly, he settled his head in between my thighs and blew. I cried out, lifted my back up off the mattress, and whimpered.

"What is it, Kayla?"

"I want you."

Drew looked up at me through hooded eyes. "Like this?"

"I want you everywhere," I replied, the words tumbling out of me. "Please, Drew. Please."

"I love it when you beg," Drew whispered, his words sending another wave of shivers racing through me. "But we're not there yet. We will be soon, though."

Abruptly, he switched his attention back to my folds and used two fingers to push them open. Then his mouth was on my center, licking and sucking until the world shifted and spun out of focus. I lifted my butt up off the mattress and twisted my legs, trying to pull him closer. Using one hand, Drew gave my legs a light smack, his focus never wavering.

Holy fuck.

He really knew what he was doing.

And I was absolutely loving every second of it, even the domineering part.

Especially that part.

As if our minds synced up with one another, Drew glanced up at me and dug his nails into either side of my thighs. This time when the orgasm came, I cried out, my moans echoing back to me, along with the smell of sweat and musty perfume. No sooner had I climbed down from the high had Drew undone my handcuffs and flipped me over. In one fluid movement, I was on my stomach, face first, into the pillow with my arms twisted behind my back.

"Is this okay? Do you want me to stop?"

I lifted my head up and craned it over my shoulder. "Don't you dare stop."

"I was hoping you would say that." Drew secured my hands behind my back and placed one leg on either side of me. I heard his sharp intake of breath, and a second later, he adjusted my ass and thrust into me in one long stroke.

My entire body was on fire.

I let out a deep and throaty moan that I barely recognized as my own. Drew placed his arms on either side of me, pumping steadily. "Yeah, baby. Uh-huh. You like it rough and dirty, don't you?"

I threw my head back and whimpered. "Mm-hmm. Just like that."

Drew pressed a kiss to the back of my neck. "I think we

should stay like this all the time. I should just stay buried inside of you, fucking you all day long."

"Fuck yes."

Drew draped his body across mine, his thrusts growing more and more frantic. "Say it, baby. I want to hear you say it."

"I want you to keep fucking me."

Drew pushed two fingers in and immediately began to stroke. "I'm going to give you the best orgasm of your life."

My eyes fluttered closed. "Oh, yes."

Over and over, he hit my sweet spot while my entire body hummed and responded to him. He played me like a fiddle, and I didn't mind at all, especially not when I heard wet sounds of his thrusts and the animalistic sounds we were making. It didn't take long for me to come again, this time with stars exploding in my field of vision. Drew gave one final thrust and emptied himself into me with a loud groan.

Afterwards, I lay in his arms, exhausted and spent. "So, when can we do that again?"

Drew chuckled and pressed a kiss to the side of my head. "I think I've created a monster."

I leaned forward and slapped his arm. "I'm serious."

Drew pressed a kiss to the side of my head. "Let's get some food, and I'll be ready for round two."

CHAPTER 2

THE NAUGHTY CHAIR

BY ALLEGRA HINES

"I can't believe you talked me into this." I shook my head and frowned in Tanner's general direction. "What else are you going to talk me into?"

Tanner smirked at me. "We've been stuck inside for a week because of the weather, so there's no time like the present."

I sighed and placed my hands on my hips. "I know that, but I feel ridiculous."

"In your French maid outfit? You look sexy as fuck." Tanner winked and strolled over to me, looking sharp and put together, in his navy suit with his dirty blonde hair brushed back. Tanner looked like he'd stepped off the cover of a major men's magazine, and I wanted nothing more than to rip his clothes off of him and spend the next few hours rolling around on the floor. As soon as the thought crossed my mind, I tilted my head back and smiled up at him. He stopped in front of me, swooped down, and gave me a deep kiss that made my toes curl.

This.

This was why I'd agreed to role-playing.

After ten years together, having met during senior year of high school and ending up in the same college through some stroke of fate, we'd weathered our fair share of storms. And as much as I hated to admit it, we were in a rut when it came to our sex life, but it was not due to a lack of passion.

Tanner still made my heart race and my knees go weak.

But I understood that he was a lot more physical than I was, so with nothing else to do on a Friday night, and no sign of the blizzard outside easing up, I figured now was a good time as any to spice up our sex life. Except I didn't know his idea of changing things up would involve costumes and rope.

It all seemed a little too much to me.

But I supposed I had nothing to lose if I tried.

With that in mind, I tugged Tanner forward, and he stumbled against me, his body warm and solid underneath my touch. He made a low noise in the back of his throat that sent a wave of desire straight to my stomach. Then he drew back and blew out a breath, his blue eyes filled with mischief.

"If you keep kissing me like that, it'll be over before it starts."

I smiled at him. "We've had our fun. Let's get to the good part."

"Trust me, when we do get there, it'll be worth it." Tanner ran his hands all over my body, leaving a trail of goosebumps in their wake. When he was done, he reached behind him and picked up a feather duster off the bed. "Here you go."

I rolled my eyes. "Do you want me to do the accent, too?"

Tanner stepped around me and gave my ass a light smack. "You bet your sweet ass I do."

The things we do for the people we love.

No sooner had the thought crossed my mind than I gave my hips a little extra sway and began to move around the room suggestively. While I did, I spoke in a ridiculous accent and kept tossing looks Tanner's way. He went from looking amused to feral, desire lurking in the depth of his eyes. I continued to bend over the chairs, the couch, and everything else within reach. Tanner stood really still and shifted from one foot to the other. When I pretended to drop the feather duster, I lingered a little with my ass hanging in the air and cast a quick look at him over my shoulder.

It turned my insides molten.

"You forgot about the chair," Tanner told me in a gruff voice. "The one in the corner."

"Oh, excusez-moi, monsieur," I said, while fluttering my lashes at him. "I did not mean to forget it."

"It's the naughty chair." Tanner flicked off the lights

before striding towards me. Seconds later, soft yellow light filled the room and gave my partner an eerier glow. "And I think you need to sit down on it."

"Have I been a bad girl?"

Tanner's hot breath was on the back of my neck when he replied. "You've been a very bad girl, and you need to be punished."

He reached over me and dragged the chair across the carpeted floor with a creek. Then he set it down so the back was facing the end of the bed. After he did that, he plucked the duster out of my hands and threw it over his shoulders. Before I knew what he was doing, he swept me into his arms and kissed me so intensely my head began to spin. Before I could deepen the kiss, however, he pushed me onto the chair, so I was straddling it. Wordlessly, he reached into his pocket and pulled out some rope. Slowly, he bent down in front of me and ran his fingers over the rope, his tongue darting out to lick his lips.

My heart skidded against my chest as he stretched my hands out and tied one to either side of the chair's leg. When he was done, he climbed onto the bed and tugged on the front of the dress impatiently. He flicked one button, then another before making a low growling noise and ripped the fabric open, allowing my breasts to spill forward. As soon as he did, Tyler stepped off the bed and came to a stand in front of me. He began to remove his shirt, his eyes never leaving my face. Before long, he stood in front of me, his naked chest glistening underneath the fluorescent lighting.

I tried to reach for him but couldn't, so I made a low whimpering noise. Tanner shot me a hungry look before lowering himself onto the bed. His eyes moved over me at a leisurely pace, taking in every inch of exposed skin before stopping at my face.

"You're so fucking hot, Jade," Tanner murmured before lowering his mouth to my nipple. His tongue swirled and moved, and I threw my head back and moaned. Tanner wasted no time in moving between the two until they were as hard as pebbles, and my breathing had grown erratic.

Abruptly, he stood up and stripped down to his boxers, revealing a tan and muscular body that my fingers itched to run all over. "Don't I get to have any fun?"

"You'll have fun," Tanner promised, his lips lifting into a half-smirk. "But tonight, I'm in charge."

"What are you going to do to me?"

Tanner came to stand behind me and ran his fingers down the length of my legs and back up, sending shivers racing up and down my spine. "I'm going to do whatever I want. You're going to like it and thank me for it, and you're going to call me sir."

I gasped when his hands came up from behind and pushed my breasts together. "Yes, sir."

"Good girl." Tanner kissed the back of my neck and ran

his tongue in lazy circles up to my earlobes and back down. "Now be a good girl and tilt your head back for me."

"Okay."

"Okay?"

"Okay, sir." I breathed and did as I was told. Tanner's body pressed against mine, while his fingers continued to tease and knead my breasts, causing the ache between my legs to grow more pronounced. Meanwhile, he alternated between kissing and biting my neck, eliciting moans and whimpers of delight. His lips parted, and he pressed hot, open-mouthed kisses along my neck, his breath sending shivers racing up and down my spine.

Holy shit.

I was suddenly really glad Tanner had talked me into this.

Without warning, Tanner pulled the rest of the dress off my body and tossed it into a heap on the floor, where it landed with a flutter. Through the walls, I heard a TV being turned up and the sound of a vacuum cleaner coming to life. Suddenly, Tanner was in front of me again, untying my hands. I watched him through hooded eyes, my throat turning dry as he brought me to my feet. Then, he used two fingers to pull down my panties, and I stepped out of them quickly, my breathing quickening. Wordlessly, he moved behind me, and gently twisted my arms behind my back, tying them both together. Gently, he coaxed me forward, so my chest was pressed against the seat of the cold, wooden chair, sending another ripple coursing through me. His hands moved up and down my bare bottom before he gave it a firm smack. A rush of pain and pleasure coursed through my veins as Tanner pressed himself against me. Suddenly, he leaned back and pressed a firm kiss to my back.

Fuck.

It felt like I was going to come right away, and my thighs clenched in response. Tanner kissed the back of my neck, leaving hot, open-mouthed kisses until I whimpered and melted further against him. When I was relaxed again, he bent down and tied each foot to a leg, leaving me completely exposed, bent over with my ass hanging in the air.

But I'd never been more turned on in my life.

"I can smell how much you want me," Tanner whispered, his voice low and husky in my ears. "You have no idea how much I want to fuck you right now. I want to bury myself in your wet pussy and fuck you all night long."

"Why aren't you, then, sir?"

"Because I want you to beg for it, first." Tanner shifted, and I went cold all over, wanting nothing more than to pull him to me and lose myself in him. Out of the corner of my eye, I saw him pull something out of a drawer and return with it. With a slow, sultry smile, he held up the feather and twisted it in his hand. My mouth parted as he climbed back onto the bed, the mattress dipping and groaning as he did. He leaned forward, his eyes fixed on my face as he touched the tip of the feather to my nipples.

The result was instant.

Tanner's eyebrows drew together as he focused on the task, tracing a path from my neck, down to my breasts and back up again, so my entire body was covered in goosebumps. When he was done, he used his tongue, his head swinging back and forth between the two until my blood turned molten, and I felt like I was going to explode. It was not long before my nipples were as hard as pebbles, and my stomach was clenched into tight knots. By now, I was sure that I was soaking wet, and I ached for him in a way I never had before.

"Tanner."

"Excuse you, who?"

Fuck.

Did he have any idea how much I wanted him right now?

"Sir, please," I begged in a strange voice. "I want you."

"How badly do you want me?" Tanner jumped off the bed and came up around me, his fingers tight around my waist. "Say it."

"I need you to fuck me right now."

Tanner placed his hands on either side of my waist, and his nails dug into my skin. "Is that all you have to say? Aren't you forgetting something?"

I blew out a breath. "I need you to fuck me right now, sir."

Tanner made a choked noise and bent me down further. "Not yet. You don't sound like you really want it."

I blew away a lock of dark hair. "But I do."

Tanner smacked my ass and dug his nails further into the sensitive flesh. "I don't think so."

Without warning, his other hand moved between us and darted into my wet pussy. Tanner wasted no time in pushing two fingers in, moving them back and forth until they were covered with my juices. I bucked and strained against the bindings, but it was no use, and the thought sent both excitement and pleasure ripping through me. He rocked his hips back and forth, his member brushing against my behind while his fingers continued to move inside of me, driving me further and further towards the edge. All at once, he switched and began to move them up and down, pressing hard as he did.

My head tilted back, and I let out a deep, throaty moan. Then I was hurtling off the cliff, wave after wave of pleasure washing over me while he held me still, his fingers still moving inside of me. I spasmed and writhed, and sweat broke out across the back of my neck, and rivulets ran down my back. Tanner's tongue lapped up the sweat until my spasms stopped, and he straightened his back again.

Damn it. I want you inside of me right now, Tyler. I want to feel that cock.

But I knew that if he said anything, he was only going to prolong the torture and take pleasure in my writhing and whimpering. By the time I could see again, and my heart was no longer pounding against my ears, I cast a quick glance over my shoulder. Tanner thrust inside of me in one quick move, his eyes going dark around the irises.

"Fuck." I breathed, squeezing my eyes shut. "That feels so good."

Tanner pushed my hair over the side of my shoulders and leaned into my back, flush and taut with desire. "You haven't seen anything yet, baby."

With that, he began to thrust, long measured strokes that filled me up while he played with my nipples. I rocked against him, meeting each thrust with a pump of my own until we were both moaning and grunting in pleasure, the sound of skin slapping against skin filling the room, along with the smell of sweat and desire. Tanner slowed and began to circle his hips, drawing out his orgasm and mine, and earning a muffled grunt in response. I twisted against my bindings, which earned me another spank, this one echoing inside of my head. Slowly, he came to a halt, eased himself out, and waited.

"Why did you stop?"

Tanner didn't respond, only slammed into me, hard. "Because I want to drag this one for as long as possible. You can't come yet."

I gasped, tears prickling my eyes. "But I'm so close."

Tanner placed his hands on either side of me and thrust again. "You can't come until I tell you to. Do you understand?"

I nodded and swallowed.

"I didn't hear you."

"I understand."

He buried himself in me and held himself absolutely still. Then, he leaned over, and his mouth was against my ear. "You understand what?"

I gasped when Tyler's hand moved to the front and pressed against my center. "I understand, sir."

Tyler lifted one hand up against the bed and grunted. "That's a good girl. Hold still, so I can fuck you long and hard."

He continued to ease out of me and slide back in, practiced and long strokes that hit all the right spots and had me breathless with anticipation. Suddenly, his pacing became frantic–animalistic, even–and his grunts grew louder as his breathing quickened. When my orgasm did come, it ripped through me with the force of a hurricane, leaving my body wracked with tremors that lasted for a few seconds. Finally, I slumped over the chair, unable to hold my weight up any longer.

Dimly, I was aware of Tanner undoing the binds and cradling me in his arms. The world shifted in and out of focus until he lowered me onto the mattress. Then he pressed a cool glass to my dry lips, and I gulped it all down, quickly. I rubbed my hands over my eyes, and he was looming over me, his hair matted to his forehead. Once I recovered my breathing, and it was no longer wheezing, I spread my legs open and beckoned him forward.

"We're not done yet."

Tanner chuckled. "Yes, ma'am."

Tanner crawled over to me, lifted my arms up over my head, and pinned them together with one palm. He reached between us, guided himself into me, and pumped in and out of me. I cried out his name, tossed my head side to side, and locked my legs together over his back. In response, Tanner's thrusts grew faster and more frenzied, forcing him to bury his face in my neck. I smelled the fresh scent of his body wash and the faint smell of sandalwood before he went absolutely still, warmth coating my center. It was not long before he rolled over next to me and tucked me into his side.

"So, what do you think?"

I tilted my head back up to look at him and gave him a small smile. "I think you owe me a massage."

Tanner chuckled and pressed a kiss to the side of my head. "Deal."

"Also, we shouldn't wait for the next snowstorm to do that."

Tanner used his thumb and forefinger to tilt my chin back. "I was hoping you'd say that. How would you feel about anime characters next time?"

CHAPTER 3

BEHIND CLOSED DOORS

BY GLENDA FITZ

Ava's body quivered all of a sudden as her index and middle fingers strayed between her plump lips. Unlike the man from the night before, the warm stream of her shower head found her clitoris with ease.

"Fuck," Ava interrupted her own moan, "I'm already late for work."

Ava never thought of herself as a sexual being, although she could have easily been mistaken for one. She was only 27 and had already experienced more than her fair share of cock. Ever since she could remember, her sexual encounters were pretty much the same: uneventful.

I'm sick of this, Ava thought as she washed from her lips the traces of John Doe's orgasm - she didn't care enough to remember his actual name.

————

"What am I doing wrong?" Ava shouted into her phone from across the room as she fixed her hair in the bathroom mirror.

"What happened?" asked Connor, her childhood friend and closest confidant.

"It's about what *didn't* happen. I couldn't orgasm."

"Was he that bad?"

"I don't know… What's bad?" Ava didn't have the slightest clue how to gauge bad sex from good. She had experienced lust. She also knew the feeling of wanting someone inside her, but once she had him in… her desire would fade.

"Okay, let me rephrase. Did he find your clit?"

"Eventually."

"Oh boy," Connor's voice flinched.

"No, it's not even that, Con," Ava interrupted, slamming her apartment door behind her. "I've had better, and it's not like I don't orgasm. Some of these guys know what they're doing, technically speaking."

"Technically speaking?" Connor asked inquisitively.

"At first, we start hot and heavy. Then, it's like," Ava paused, looking for the right words as she drove out of her parking space. "I don't know. I just stop feeling pleasure. Sure, my body feels stimulated, excited, whatever. My mind, though…"

"It's off somewhere, thinking about what you're gonna have for lunch tomorrow?"

"Exactly," Ava snapped.

"I see." Connor sounded preoccupied. "I know you don't do relationships, and you might want to see a therapist about that-"

"Connor," Ava warned.

"I know what you're feeling. I felt the same way with the girls, who came after Jessica."

"I never had a Jessica."

"You're taking it literally," Connor paused. "Maybe the problem isn't them. It's you."

Ava felt herself getting defensive even before she spoke. "Maybe." She restrained herself. "I've got to go now, Con."

"Are you okay? I'm sorry if I-"

"I'm fine," Ava's curt reply suggested otherwise. "I just need to get my shit together before I go into work."

"Can you wait? Please." Silence followed Connor's words. "What?"

"I didn't mean that something is wrong with you," Connor explained. "I meant... okay, don't shut down this idea without hearing it out first. Deal?"

"Connor, get to the point."

"Rachel. The girl from work you set me up with."

"Whom I didn't know wasn't into guys, yes?"

"Great. Do you remember acting differently that night?"

"Not really," Ava ruffled through her memories.

"Well, you were both very," Connor paused, "comfort-able around each other, and not in a platonic sense."

"What? When? At the bar?"

"Was there anywhere else?" Connor burst.

"What are you? Twelve? Your gender's fragile masculinity doesn't define the rest of us."

"Ouch," he interjected.

"It's normal to touch your friends. It doesn't have to mean more than that."

"Look, here's what I know. You don't know what good sex is. No matter how bad you want to get laid, you lose interest five minutes in. Last, but definitely not least, you don't feel *pleasure* while being *pleasured*."

Ava's chest felt heavy under the weight of Connor's very compelling points. She'd mulled over the possibility a few times after particularly bland sex. The thought, however, scared her more than she liked to admit. It felt similar to making a complete career shift after achieving a senior position.

"Ava? Still here?"

"Yeah... I don't know, Connor," Ava finally replied. "I don't want to open this door, and I seriously need to go now."

"Okay, buddy," said Connor, "I'm here if you ever do open it."

"Thanks."

"Have a nice day." The expression came out sounding more like a question.

"Yeah. You, too."

———

What am I doing? Ava caught herself slowly stroking her black office keyboard. The pleasant memory of her shower-head from earlier came rushing in.

On any other day, Ava would have been able to distract herself, but the job was much harder with no ongoing projects to keep her busy. She had just submitted her last marketing campaign, so she had to wait for her turn in the rotation.

Can I get fired for masturbating in the bathroom? Ava's nose involuntarily crinkled. *Shit, I'm a pervert in the making.*

Ava looked up from her screen and around her office. Everyone seemed too busy to notice her. Her hand reached for her phone, and she quietly walked off.

Phone-in-hand, she walked into the warmly-lit bathroom, past the three empty stalls, and into the fourth.

"Wait," hissed a soft, distant voice.

About to lock the door, Ava froze in place for a second as the voice called out again. This time, however, it was much clearer than the one before.

"Rachel?" Ava opened the door and stepped out.

"Babe." Rachel clung to Ava's hands. "Could you check me?" Her distressed eyes implored Ava.

"Check you?" Ava asked.

Rachel nodded frantically. "For lumps. I thought I found one this morning, but then I lost it, and now I'm spiraling."

Unable to say no, Ava reluctantly replied, "Umm... I guess."

She bid adieu her chance at getting off as she followed Rachel into the narrow stall.

Rachel's long, slender fingers worked their way around the buttons of her cream shirt, slowly revealing the mounds of her supple breasts. Her floral scent filled the warm air between her and Ava who, up until that point, had had her gaze politely averted.

The scent overpowered Ava, however, forcing her eyes to Rachel's soft, honey-colored skin. Heat bubbled in Ava's chest, followed by unbridled anticipation as Rachel reached backward to unhook her bra.

"Are you okay?" Rachel asked, noticing the redness in Ava's cheeks only inches away from her.

"I'm... yeah, I'm fine," Ava stammered. *What the hell is going on?* Ava barked at herself, *Get it together, Ava. Why is this weird? They're just boobs. You have them, too.*

Rachel's bra sank ever so slightly under the weight of her breasts. Ava's gaze shifted to Rachel's face—a desperate attempt to stop herself from staring at Rachel's nipples.

"Okay." Rachel's soft, concerned eyes met Ava's tense gaze. "I'm ready."

Ava opened her mouth, but no words came out. She looked into Rachel's anxiety-stricken eyes, then down at her plump bottom lip, and all the way to her perked-up nipples. She bit the inside of her cheek as she felt a sudden wetness between her thighs.

"Rachel," Ava stammered, "I can't do this."

"Why not?" Rachel furrowed her eyebrows.

"I..." Ava inhaled deeply.

"You're not into women," stated Rachel.

"I don't know." Ava shrugged her shoulders. "I'm feeling... It's very complicated. Connor, remember him? We were talking today, and he said some-"

Rachel's eyes slightly lost their edge, and her lips curled into a subtle smile. "Are you turned on by me?"

The question caught her off-guard. She could already feel the tension building up as she looked into Rachel's wide eyes. Rachel's expression changed, from distressed to hungry, and it sent a shock straight to Ava's stomach. Her throat felt dry as she struggled to swallow past the sudden lump in her throat.

"I—I, I don't know."

She turned away from Rachel and ignored the heat pooling in her body and the color rising up her cheeks. "Look, I'm sorry...."

"Why are you apologizing?"

Rachel came to a stop behind Ava and pressed her bare breasts against her back. The feel of them pressed against Ava's back did something strange to her insides. And when Rachel's mouth parted and pressed a hot, open-mouthed kiss to the back of her neck, her knees buckled. Rachel grazed the back of her skin, her mouth sending shivers of delight racing up and down Ava's spine.

Holy Shit.

Was Connor right?

Was the problem that she wasn't into men at all?

As soon as the thought crossed her mind, Rachel's hand came up around her chest and squeezed. "How does that feel?"

Ava swallowed. "It feels amazing."

Rachel removed her hand and took a step back. "You're easily the most beautiful woman around here, and the sexiest, and when you told me you want to set me up with someone, I thought it was me."

Ava spun around to face her, her heart racing against her chest. "You did?"

"I hoped it was," Rachel whispered, taking a step closer. "But I don't want Connor, Ava. I hope I've made that clear by now."

"Oh."

Rachel bit her lower lip and ran a finger across one of her bare nipples. "Are you wet for me?"

The words drove Ava crazy. She'd lost the grip on her

mind as her urges took over. Her lips longed to caress Rachel's hardened nipples. Her stomach clenched and tightened, and she found herself drifting closer to the redheaded temptress.

This is how it should feel. Fuck. Ava is driving me crazy, and she hasn't even touched me.

"It's okay," Rachel interrupted Ava's thinking process with a tender smile. "Let me show you how it goes."

Before she could reply, Rachel pulled Ava towards her. Quickly, she slipped her fingers under Ava's blouse. Ava's skin tingled with Rachel's every touch, sending waves from the small of her back and up her spine. Every touch was electric, and every part of Ava came alive in a way it never had before.

And she wanted more.

"Fuck me." The words escaped Ava's lips before they were quickly replaced with a soft moan.

Rachel gave her a slow, sultry smile before cupping her hands around Ava's firm breasts, her thumbs hovering over Ava's pink, wanting nipples. Ava's back arched with a wave of electricity at Rachel's first flick.

"Do you want more?" Rachel's warm breath fell soft against Ava's porcelain neck.

"Yeah."

Rachel's thumbs worked Ava's nipples, rubbing them up and down. Gently, at first, then faster in response to Ava's demanding moans. Ava drew a sharp breath as she felt

Rachel's tongue going up her neck and behind her earlobe. Swiftly, the wet warmth of Rachel's mouth surrounded Ava's earlobe.

Ava's mound shot upwards, yearning for Rachel's touch to fill the emptiness between her thighs. Rachel's hands swiftly moved from Ava's breasts to her waist. She guided her to the covered toilet before straddling her.

"Relax, baby," Rachel whispered in her ear.

"Touch me," Ava begged.

Rachel tutted. "In time, I'll make you come hard."

lowered her head and took Ava's right nipple between her lips and into her mouth.

Ava couldn't comprehend what Rachel's lightning-quick tongue was doing to her, but every flick of that soft tongue on her aching nipple sent heat waves from between her legs. She struggled to suppress her moans. Each passing second pushed Ava closer to the edge, and Rachel's soft pull on her nipples didn't help.

Rachel had her fingertips firmly planted around Ava's left nipple, threatening to pinch her soft pink flesh. Ava's chest thrust inwards, and a short, sharp moan penetrated their hushed bubble.

Rachel's mouth briskly replaced her hand on Ava's left nipple, kissing the now-reddened flesh. Once again, Ava's mound rose, yearning for Rachel's touch, and even more so as the towering goddess above her reached to unbutton her pants.

Ava arched her back to receive Rachel's dry fingers between her plump lips, soaked in anticipation. Softly, Rachel parted Ava's fleshy lips, exposing her dripping warmth. Ava let out a soft, hushed moan at Rachel's touch. Her middle finger circled the cusp of Ava's flesh, teasing her senses before it ran up to her pulsating clit.

Ava sank in her seat, releasing a long, sigh-like moan. She gasped and moaned at Rachel's every touch. Her finger's movements, gentle and slow at first, but gradually growing more frantic and exact, sent waves of escalating pleasure through Ava's fragile body.

Lick my nipples, the thought involuntarily erupted from Ava's mind.

Rachel leaned forward, entangling her tongue with Ava's left nipple, each lick followed by a passionate suckling, ending with a kiss. She cradled Ava's right breast with her free hand, tracing around her nipple with her thumb before rubbing her erect flesh.

"Yeah," Ava's whisper turned to a moan. "Yeah." Heat surged through her body, and sweat trickled down her back. She hadn't been fucked like that before. Her vagina ached to be filled with Rachel's slender, slithering fingers. Her unwavering clit demanded Rachel's steady stroke. The fire in her nipples craved the relief of Rachel's moist tongue.

Ava let go of her eyelids, losing herself in the darkness, grounding herself in the bubbling sensations.

"You like that?" Rachel whispered, grinding up on Ava as she did, nearing her breasts to Ava's face.

Ava moaned in reply.

"Then how about you suck on me, too, pillow princess?"

Ava opened her eyes to see Rachel's playful smirk directly above her and her heavy breasts inches away from her mouth. She let go of Rachel's behind, moving her hands up Rachel's stomach, and arriving at her supple mounds.

With mixed feelings, a sense of uncertainty, and a hunger she'd never felt before, Ava filled her hands with Rachel's breasts and buried her face in their softness. Rachel's scent filled Ava's nostrils as she jumped from breast to breast, kissing their delicate flesh.

Is this working? Ava hoped for an answer or some guidance. She knew what she liked, but being with another woman was completely out of her depth.

"Yeah, baby," Rachel grunted. She rubbed Ava's clit faster in approval.

A sweet shock ran down Ava's spine. Her body jerked with pleasure, but swiftly her tongue found one of Rachel's dark, erect nipples. She pushed against the firm nipple with her tongue and felt it hit her lower lip as it snapped back into place. One lick after the other, Ava hungrily persisted.

"I could lick them until they're raw," said Ava between gasps.

"So lick them." Rachel pushed her breasts against Ava's face.

Ava's uncertain grip on Rachel's breasts firmed. Her tongue rubbed against Rachel's nipples with a newfound intensity.

Rachel gritted her teeth, letting out short gasps instead of loud moans. "Where did you get a tongue like that?" She gripped the wall with her free hand for balance. "I might need to make you come before you make me scream."

"So, make me." Ava's lips curled into a devious smile.

Rachel slightly tilted her head, clearly impressed. "You asked for it."

In a few seconds, Ava's pants and panties were on the ground, and Rachel was kneeling between her legs. Ava released a hushed moan as she felt Rachel's warm breath on her pussy.

Ava's lips parted wide to make way for a louder moan when she felt Rachel's velvet tongue on her wet flesh. Instinctively, Ava bit the inside of her cheek to silence herself.

Meanwhile, Rachel was hard at work. Her full lips surrounded Ava's pussy, and her tongue carried the soft clit into the warmth of her mouth. Ava's body jerked, putting a smile on Rachel's face.

Ava's teeth clamped on the inside of her cheek when she felt Rachel's hand near her opening. Suddenly, her body loosened to receive Rachel's finger in her warm wetness. In and out, Rachel thrust her middle finger before she intro-duced a second. Euphoria bubbled inside Ava's chest every time she felt Rachel's gentle, persistent pressure against her wanting flesh.

All the while, Rachel's tongue writhed around Ava's clit. Her mouth dripped with Ava's water as her tongue licked her enlarged clit raw.

"Don't stop," Ava gasped and thrust her pussy upward. With a shudder, she took in Rachel's fingers and buried her clit in Rachel's mouth as her water kept flowing.

Rachel's tongue frantically rubbed against Ava's clit while her fingers moved in circles inside her. Ava's body jerked backward, but Rachel's pace wasn't thrown off.

The euphoria build-up in Ava's chest was getting too much to bear. Once more, her body quivered, and her clenched muscles burned.

"I'm gonna come," she whispered urgently.

With each passing second, ecstasy built up and, with it, a sense of tension. Ava ached for a release, and it was close. She gasped sharply, and her body quivered. She lost control over her thigh muscles as they clenched to the point of unbearable pain. With a sudden jerk, her muscles unclenched. Ava let go, surrendering herself to the waves of pleasure and the sweet release.

She furrowed her eyebrows and let out a groan as her warm come flowed out, drenching Rachel's mouth and fingers.

Rachel leaned back, smiling. "You taste as good as you look."

Ava sighed, wanting to reply, unable to speak.

"Take your time, babe." Rachel picked up her shirt and put it on. "Maybe, thank Connor, too."

"What?" Ava sat up straight.

"I'm not stupid. I didn't *need* you to check me, Ava." A playful smile drew on Rachel's face. "I felt a certain way about you. Connor confirmed my suspicions. I thought I'd help you, erm... see the light."

With a wink, Rachel exited the stall, leaving the confused Ava to wrap her head around everything.

CHAPTER 4
HAPPY ANNIVERSARY
BY CHARLES SERRA

"I was thinking we could stay in tonight." Amelia reached behind me and slammed the door shut. "What do you think?"

I raised an eyebrow. "I thought you wanted to go out."

"I did." My wife peeled off her coat and threw it onto the floor next to me. "But I want to spend some time with you."

I tugged on my tie and cleared my throat. "We are spending time together."

Amelia smiled at me and leaned forward. "I know, but I had something... else in mind."

My grin stretched from ear to ear. "Does this mean we're not in a rut anymore?"

"Honey, we've been married for 10 years now, and I thought about what you've been saying. You're right. We should try something new."

I removed the tie and rolled up the sleeves of my shirt. "So, you made me get dressed up for nothing?" I said playfully.

Amelia pushed herself up to the tips of her toes and kissed me. "You look incredibly sexy in your suit, so it's not for nothing."

I smiled into the kiss and kicked off my shoes. "Does this mean you're actually ready to try something... different?"

She coyly nodded as her hand ran down the nape of her neck and gently caressed her perfect tits. "We *could* do something... different."

She didn't have to say it out loud; I knew what she meant. Last week, on our anniversary, I'd opened up about a fantasy I'd been holding onto for years

Nothing complicated; we didn't need costumes or props. I simply wanted to fuck my wife in the ass.

"Why don't we try some dirty talk first to get in the mood?"

I nodded and pulled her closer to me. "Fuck, yes!"

"I love feeling your hands all over me," whispered Amelia, color rushing into her cheeks. Then, she took my hands and led me to the couch. "You are the sexiest man on the planet, Paul."

Then, like she was presenting herself to me for the first time, she slowly and methodically slipped off her dress, letting it drop to the floor, revealing her stunning, voluptuous body totally naked.

I swallowed and said, "Even after all these years, I look at the curves of your body and think - wow - every moment I'm not touching you is torture."

Slowly, she pushed me onto the couch and climbed on top of me. With one leg on either side of me, she ground against me. "There's nowhere else I'd rather be than on top of you right now."

I ran my hands along the length of her and stopped at the small of her back. Without warning, I thrust upwards, all the blood rushing south and straining against the fabric of my pants.

"Yeah? Having me under you is good," I said, "but isn't it even better when I'm inside you?"

Amelia leaned forward and pressed her bare chest against me. My breath hitched in my throat as her hands moved down, touching me through the thin fabric of my pants. Then, she pressed a kiss to the side of his neck and licked a path up to my ear.

"I want you to cum so hard that I feel your cock pulsing inside me," she murmured before giving my earlobe a quick tug."

"Inside you?" I pulled back to make sure we were on the same page. Had I misunderstood what we were about to do?

Amelia pulled me to my feet, led me a few steps away from the couch, and gave me a sultry look. Then, with a confidence I'm not used to from her, she slowly rotated her body without ever losing eye contact. She was looking over her shoulder as she caressed her gorgeous ass, her hair cascading down her back.

"Happy Anniversary," she said.

Fuck, yes.

I came up behind her, and she gingerly leaned over, putting her hand on the arm of the sofa. I started to kiss her neck, which I know she loves, but with a little more force than usual. What can I say? I was excited.

When she heard me fumble with my belt buckle, Amelia quickly turned around, put one hand on my crotch, and started to speak. "We can't forget-"

I interrupted her. "The lube. Shit, where is it?" Amelia shifted her

weight just enough to reach over to the drawer in the table next to the couch... which is not where the lube is usually stored. Fuck, she is pulling all the strings tonight, and I love it.

I wouldn't say I'm an expert in this area, but I have done it a few times. She was an anal virgin. So, I had to be slow and gentle; let her get accustomed to the sensation before I fuck her so hard she'll be screaming her head off.

I took off my clothes. You could practically hear my cock sigh to be released from the prison of my underwear. Amelia, starting to show a little nervousness, spun around again, hands on the couch. She had assumed the position.

Amelia was the sexiest woman I'd ever seen, and I wanted her to enjoy every minute of this. I pressed up behind her, my hard dick slickly sliding on her lower back. She let out a satisfied moan. The first of many tonight, I hoped.

I moved my left hand to her front, caressing her breasts, and as my other hand moved down the crack of her ass. I gently placed my lubed finger on her asshole. To my surprise, she didn't flinch. In fact, she took a deep breath and pushed back gently. Little by little, she was relaxing against my finger, so I could push inside. She let out another soft moan and took another deep breath. I kissed her neck softly as she was getting used to the sensation. When she gave me a little nod, I squirted a little more lube on my hand and worked in a second finger. Her moan changed, and she started to make this animalistic noise that I'd never heard before. But fuck, did I enjoy it.

After a few seconds, she straightened up a little and looked over her shoulder at me, my fingers still in her hole. I gently began to move them in and out.

Her eyes widened, and a wicked smile appeared on her face. "That feels fucking great."

In an uncharacteristic show of bravado, I replied, "Yeah? Well, imagine how good my cock is going to feel?"

Amelia sucked in a deep breath and nodded. "I'm ready to find out."

I stood up straighter, positioned myself behind her, and eased my lubed cock into her ass. When Amelia's muscles clenched, and she went still, I stopped. "I'll hold right here. You tell me when you're ready."

Amelia inhaled deeply, let out that animal moan again - fuck that makes me hard - and said, "Give me a minute."

"I love that noise you make when I'm inside of your ass, babe," I told her in a low and confident voice.

Amelia went silent for a second and simply said, "Keep going."

Yes, ma'am.

Slowly, I thrust in further and waited. Amelia gasped and tensed again. Using every ounce of energy and self-control I had, I kept myself completely still and dug my nails into the inside of my palms.

As soon as Amelia sighed, I eased out of her for a moment and moved back in, as carefully as possible. Amelia gasped and clenched her hands into fists. "Fuck, you're so big."

"Do you want me to stop?"

Amelia shook her head. "Fuck, no. Keep going."

With a smile, I pulled out of her and eased back, going further and further each time. I kept sliding in and out of her until Amelia's breath quickened and sweat formed on the back of her neck. Then, she threw her head backward, and her muscles clenched around me. Suddenly, I placed both of my hands against her back and thrust all the way in.

Amelia pushed backward, and I squeezed my eyes shut.

Together, the two of us moved, back and forth, skin slapping against skin until her entire body grew relaxed. It wasn't long before Amelia was moaning and whimpering, the sound reverberating inside my head. Of their own accord, my hands fell on either side of her hips and dug into the sensitive skin there. While she moved backward, I kept her caged in, entirely at mercy.

It was the hottest thing I'd ever experienced. Fucking my wife in the ass.

Immediately, my eyes flew open, and I studied her back and the rivulets of sweat glistening across her tanned skin. My mouth parted, and I leaned forward, pausing to run my tongue over her skin. She tasted like soap and something floral I couldn't identify, and I allowed it to wash over me. I brought one of my hands around to her pussy, and gently started to do that thing I do with my finger that she loves, while I continued to rhythmically fuck her.

Over and over, I pushed her closer to the edge, taking pleasure in feeling every inch of her until she writhed and spasmed. Amelia repeated my name a few times, her voice growing weaker and weaker while she struggled to catch her breath. Then, she released a deep breath followed by that moan. That fucking moan that was driving me crazy with lust.

I gave one final thrust and came. Hard. In my wife's ass. Fuck, yes.

———

"I have to go back to work."

Amelia tilted her head back to look at me and pouted. "But we have time before you have to be there."

I checked my watch. "We do, but I wanted to get there early."

Amelia raised an eyebrow. "Why?"

"Because I've got some paperwork to finish."

Amelia sat back on her legs and peeled off her shirt. She tossed it onto the bed next to her and reached behind her back. When her breasts spilled forward, my mouth turned dry, and all the blood rushed to my groin. Riveted, I stood rooted to the spot as she removed the rest of her clothing until she was stark naked. Afterwards, she spun around and lifted herself up on her hands and knees.

"I fucking love you and your perfect dick."

With my heart pounding in my ears, I hurried out of my shirt. Then, I hopped around, trying to get rid of my trousers. By the time they came off, Amelia was already fingering her ass and moaning.

Fuck.

I guess I'm going to be late to work.

Quickly, I hopped onto the bed, which creaked and groaned underneath me, and positioned myself at her entrance. Amelia stopped and craned her neck over her shoulder, offering me a slow and sultry smile.

"Tell me you want me."

"I want to fuck you until I can feel that sweet little pussy clenching around my cock."

Amelia sighed. "

Pussy? How boring."

"Amelia, you animal."

Amelia nodded. "It just feels so good."

While I enjoyed spicing up our sex life and exploring new territory with my wife, I wasn't expecting her to like it so much. As if she sensed my hesitation, Amelia wriggled her ass in my face and made a soft version of that moan I love. Amelia handed me the bottle of lube. (Had she been hiding this all morning?) A moment later, I positioned myself behind her and thrust in. Fuck, it felt good.

I thought, What if she only wanted to have anal sex from now on?

Considering how good it felt, I could think of worse things. So, I pushed the thought out of my mind and focused on the feel of her wrapped around me. Before long, she was grinding against me, and making that noise that makes my blood boil. Eventually, I reached for one of her arms and twisted it behind her back. She used her free arm to keep herself balanced before bringing it to a rest against the headboard.

I eased in and out of her in quick succession, earning a groan each time. Before long, Amelia had her head tossed back, and her back was covered in sweat. I bent my head down and licked a path up to her neck. Then, I sat back on my legs and thrust upwards, wanting to feel as much of her as possible.

Amelia continued to thrust backward. Through the mirror, standing near the bed, I saw her free hand push her breasts together. Abruptly, I released her other hand and watched, transfixed, as her fingers darted in between her wet folds. She rubbed herself furiously, color tainting her cheeks.

Hold it in, Paul. Come on. It's only been a few minutes, and she looks like she could go all night.

Suddenly, Amelia froze, threw her head back, and cried out. Her body writhed and spasmed against me while her orgasm ripped through her. I listened to the sound of her heavy breathing and gave a few more thrusts before shooting my load myself into her. When I was done, I collapsed against the mattress and brought my hands up over my head.

"That was intense."

"I don't know why you didn't introduce me to anal before." Amelia curled herself around me and threw one leg up over me. "I'm definitely enjoying it."

I pressed a kiss to the side of her head. "I can see that."

Amelia tilted her head back to look up at me. "Does that bother you?"

I shook my head. "No, it doesn't bother me, but there are other options."

Amelia lifted her head up and frowned. "So, you don't like anal anymore?"

"I absolutely fucking do. But it's not all I want to do with you."

Amelia smiled. "We can do more... experimenting."

I pulled her back next to me and kissed her cheek. "Good because there are a few more things I had in mind."

Amelia giggled and placed a hand over my chest. "Yeah, like what?"

"Role-playing, a threesome."

"A threesome with another woman?"

I twisted my head to look at her and nodded. "You bet your ass. Imagine you and another woman, absolutely naked and covered in water."

"Why are we covered in water?"

"Because you're in a Jell-O pool."

Amelia snorted. "Are you being serious? This sounds like a bad porno."

I ran my hands along her arm, and goosebumps broke out across her skin. "You said that about anal too. You'll never know unless you try."

"You're definitely right, but if we do go through with that, I get to pick the woman."

"As long as you're both wearing lacy clothing, I'm in."

"And I'll think about the Jell-O thing."

I laughed. "Fair enough. Maybe I can get one of those inflatable pools, and we can fill it with chocolate pudding."

Amelia slapped my arm. "God, are you always so...."

"Creative? Resourceful?"

"Pervy," Amelia teased, pausing to stick her tongue out. "Get your head out of the gutter."

"Never. I've got a hot, naked woman in my bed, and all I want to do is find a way to make her make that moaning noise I love. Why would I want to get my head out of the gutter?"

Amelia laughed and kissed me. "When you put it like that, you make a good point."

I twisted onto my side and pressed myself against her.

"Babe, what noise do I make?"

"Amelia, do you not even know you moan like that?"

She hit me with a pillow. "Oh my god, what noise do I make?"

"I guess I'll have to show you. Flip over for round two."

CHAPTER 5

THE HIGH FIVE

BY SHANICE WARREN

I folded my arms over my chest and looked between the two of them. "I know this is weird, but I thought it was the best way to resolve this."

Damien glanced up at the ceiling and back at my face. "So, you want to solve this love triangle by having sex?"

"Yes."

"With the two of us?" Joshua added with a frown. "That doesn't sound like a good idea at all. It sounds like a recipe for disaster."

I shrugged. "I don't agree. I think the three of us could have a lot of fun."

Joshua ran a hand over his face. "Amber, I think you're great, and we have a lot of fun together, but there's no need to add another guy into the mix."

"It sounds like you're not doing it for her," Damien muttered under his breath.

"What did you just say?"

Damien twisted his head and gave Joshua a bored look. "You guys have been dating for weeks, and she's already looking to someone else for pleasure."

Joshua frowned. "It has nothing to do with it."

"It doesn't," I pointed out with a smile. "I just want to try something new and spice things up."

Silence stretched between us.

Given that I'd lured them both here under false pretenses, it was only natural that they were both hesitant. On the one hand, Joshua was the strong and successful kind, who spent most of his time behind his desk, barking out orders and looking like a male model in his custom-made suits. Damien, on the other hand, was the brooding artistic kind who spent most of his time in his studio, hunched over an easel with paint stains all over his shirts.

As far as I was concerned, they both did it for me.

But now it was time to mix and match.

All I needed was to show them how much fun it could be.

I licked my lips in anticipation. "We don't have to do this if you guys don't want to, but I think we could all enjoy this."

Joshua cleared his throat. "How would this work?"

"I'm glad you asked." I paused and kicked the door shut with the back of my leg. The thud sounded through the apartment, but I ignored it and pulled my shirt up over my head. After tossing it onto the floor, I walked over to the window and gave my hips a little extra sway. I pulled the curtains shut and spun around to face them with a slow, sultry smile.

Both of them were rooted to the spot, right where I wanted them.

So, I placed one hand on my hips while the other undid the hooks of my bra. As soon as my breasts spilled forward, Joshua's eyes widened, and Damien shifted on his feet. I looked from one man to the other and pushed my breasts together. Abruptly, I stopped, spun around, and bent over. I heard Joshua's sharp intake of breath as I unbuttoned my jeans and slid them down over my ass, taking my sweet time. By the time I had spun around, I was naked except for a lace thong covering my nether regions.

Damien's eyes were dark with hunger, and Joshua's hands were clenched into fists at his side. "The door is over there, boys. Whenever you want to leave. No one is keeping you here."

Joshua swallowed. "You're so fucking hot."

"And sexy," Damien replied in a husky voice. "I love a woman who knows what she wants."

"Do we need to establish some ground rules?"

Damien and Joshua exchanged a quick look before inching away from each other. I placed my hands on my hips and smiled. "Neither of you have to do anything with each other if you're not comfortable. Do whatever feels right."

Josh tugged on his collar and cleared his throat. "That sounds fair."

"Agreed," Damien added in a louder voice. "I'm in."

Joshua stood up straighter, and his eyes moved over me, leaving a trail of heat in their wake. "Me too."

Wordlessly, I pointed a finger at Damien and beckoned him forward. He strolled over to me, placed both hands on my hips, and kissed me. The room spun and shifted out of focus, and my blood turned molten. Then he wrenched his lips away and peppered my neck with hot, open-mouthed kisses. I stepped backward, and my back collided with the cold, hard wall.

Damien growled into the kiss. "After this, you're going to realize I'm the only man you'll ever need."

I smiled and pulled back. "We'll see."

Slowly, I looked over at Joshua and cocked a finger in his direction. He hesitated, then walked over to me. I unhooked my arms from around Damien and spun around to face Joshua, whose green eyes were full of hunger. He cupped my face in his hands and brushed his mouth against mine. His kiss was feather-light and restrained until I nipped on his lower lip, and he made a low growling noise. Our tongues began a sensual battle for dominance while Joshua's arms moved up and down mine, leaving chills everywhere he touched.

Fuck.

He sure did know how to make a woman ache for more.

Suddenly, I was pressed against him with his erection pressed up against my center. My lips curved into a smile as I ground against him and earned myself a throaty moan in response. Then his hands were moving up and down my sides again while I fumbled with his belt. When I finally undid the loops, I leaned back and pushed his jeans down to his ankles. While he unbuttoned his shirt, I twisted to face Damien, who was already naked and standing underneath the fluorescent lights. His tan and naked body glistened, and my throat turned dry at the sight.

He looked right at home in the middle of my living room.

Although I had no idea how I'd managed to convince the two of them to go through with this, I wasn't about to go questioning my methods. Especially not when they worked. So, I rose up to my feet, and my eyes danced between the two, my breathing turning even.

Both of them looked directly at my heaving breasts.

Through the thin walls, I could hear the distant sound of the TV, interrupted by the occasional rise and fall of conversation. With a shake of my head, I took Damien's hand and led him to the couch. I pushed him down and placed one leg on either side of him. His hands immediately went to my ass and squeezed, his warm, calloused fingers leaving a trail of heat in their wake. Our lips collided together, and I inhaled his taste -peppermint and beer - and allowed it to fill me.

Once the need for air became too great, I threw my head back and moaned. Damien took one nipple between his teeth and pulled. He did the same to the other one, so they were both as hard as pebbles, and my heart was pounding in my ears.

Joshua came to stand behind me, his hot breath searing against my bare back. Then, his hands came up around my breasts, flicking and twisting. I squeezed my eyes shut and let out a deep, throaty groan. Josh's lips found my neck, and he sucked on the sensitive skin there, sending wave after wave of desire pulsing through me. I pried my eyes open, leaned back, and stood up. After motioning for Joshua to sit down next to Damien, I came to a stop in front of them. Their attention was solely on me, and the hungry expressions on their faces almost had me bending over and urging them to have their way with me.

Be patient. I know you want both of them inside of you, but if you want this to last for as long as possible, you have to get creative. Show them both what they'll be enjoying.

Instead, using one hand, I pushed down my thong, and with the other one, I fingered myself.

Josh and Damien's mouths fell open.

I kept my gaze fixed on their faces while I continued to touch myself, moving faster and faster until my finger was covered with my own juices. When I saw Damien get up, I stopped and stared at him through hooded eyes. Wordlessly, he knelt down on the carpet in front of me, and his head disappeared between my legs. His long, expert tongue moved back and forth while his hot breath danced against my sensitive skin. I tilted my head back, threaded my fingers through his hair, and tightened. I let out a deep, husky moan and pressed myself against him, wanting more.

My orgasm ripped through me, leaving me panting and breathless.

When Damien came back up, a smirk hovering on the edge of his lips, I pulled him in for a kiss. Then I looked over his shoulder at Joshua and motioned to him. He jumped off the couch and walked over to me, tan skin glistening with sweat. I ran my hands along Damien's shoulders and down his back, pausing at his ass and giving it a light squeeze.

"How about we kick things up a notch?"

Joshua and Damien exchanged a quick look. "What do you mean?"

I spun around to face Joshua and wrapped both hands around his neck. When I drew him closer and felt his erection pressing against me, my pulse quickened. "I want you to fuck me, Josh."

Josh's lips parted. "You have no idea how much I want you right now."

My hand fell between us and squeezed. "I think I have some idea."

Joshua kept one hand on the back of my neck while the other slid down the curve of my back and came to a rest on top of my ass. He gave it a light slap. "How do you want me to fuck you?"

Without warning, I wheeled around, lowered myself onto my knees, and leaned forward. "I want you to fuck me from the back."

Josh released a deep breath. "Fuck, yes, baby."

I lifted my gaze and held Damien's. "And I want to suck on your cock. You'd like that, right?"

Damien grinned. "Fuck, yes."

I placed my hands on either side of the carpet and waited, my heart thundering against my chest. Briefly, I wondered if I'd bitten off more than I could chew, setting myself up for failure, but before I could dwell on it any further, Joshua lowered himself onto the carpet and entered me from behind.

Holy shit.

My muscles tightened and clenched around him until he was all the way in. As soon as he was, I ground against him and whimpered. "Oh, God, yes. That feels so good."

Damien came to a stop in front of me and wound his fingers through my hair. Quickly, he got down on his knees and positioned himself in front of me. "You haven't seen anything yet."

I tilted my head back and gave him a smile. Then I bent down and began to lick him. I ran my tongue along one side, then the other, before I took him inside of my mouth. After releasing a deep breath, I began to suck.

Damien threw his head back and groaned loudly.

The sound reverberated inside my head and made my

stomach clench even further. Red hot desire sliced through my veins, and a familiar feeling began to bubble up within me. Damien's grip on my hair tightened.

Meanwhile, Joshua began to move inside of me, long, smooth strokes while his nails dug into my skin. He dug his nails even further, sending a wave of pain and pleasure ricocheting through me. Josh pressed a kiss to the middle of my back, eased out, and slammed back in. A wave of pleasure crashed into me, and I squeezed my eyes shut. He continued to thrust, in and out, getting faster and faster until the sound of skin slapping against skin reverberated against my ears.

Damien's grip tightened on my hair, and I groaned.

Together, the three of us moved in sync, taking and giving in equal pleasure. Between Damien's cock in my mouth and Joshua's inside of me, it felt like I was going to explode. Every inch of me was on fire, like I was going to explode into a million pieces. The pressure built up within me, growing stronger until Damien's hands reached down and kneaded my breasts.

I yelped in response. "Holy shit."

"That's it, baby," Joshua growled into my ears. His hot breath sent ripples breaking out all over my skin. "You like that, don't you?"

"You're so fucking hot," Damien told me in a thick voice. "I could do this all night."

My eyes squeezed shut, and I focused on my movements, alternating between bouncing back and forth and moving my tongue around. I felt Joshua shift, and his movements became frantic like he'd lost all control, and it made my stomach tighten in response. Suddenly, Damien's pace changed too, and he moved in and out of my mouth, and I peeked one eye open to see his muscles rippling. Out of the corner of my eye, I caught a quick glimpse of us in the floor-length living room mirror, and I nearly came right then and there.

It was the most erotic thing I'd ever done, and I was loving every minute of it.

No sooner had the thought crossed my mind had my pulse quickened, and I went hurtling over the edge. As soon as I caught my breath, Joshua eased out of me and emptied himself onto the carpet. Then Damien pulled up on shaky feet and towards the couch. With a wicked smile, he pulled me on top of him and thrust inward.

I arched my back and tossed my head back. "*Fuck.* Oh, God. You guys are going to kill me."

Damien slammed into me and buried his face in my neck. While he moved, Joshua panted somewhere behind me, and it made my knees go weak. Abruptly, Damien reached up and claimed my mouth with his, his lips hot and searing and demanding every inch of me. Another wave built up within me, growing stronger and stronger with each passing second.

I squeezed my eyes shut, threw my head back, and focused on Damien's cock inside of me, filling every inch of me. Without warning, I felt Joshua come up behind me, his quick and nimble fingers moving over the length of my back and pausing at the curve of my ass. Then, they moved back up and around to my breasts, pressing them together. Joshua pressed his lips to the back of my neck and bit down, hard.

Slowly, I leaned into Joshua's touch and twisted my arms over my head, touching as much of him as I could. He removed his hands and traced my back while Damien reached up between us and cupped my breasts between his hands. I could feel Joshua's eyes on me as he bent down and took one nipple between his teeth. When he reached for the other, rivulets of sweat began to pour down my back and down the slope of my chest. Joshua's growl sent another wave of desire through me.

Before long, another orgasm washed over me, this time making me spasm and shake until my lungs burned. When he was done, Damien eased out of me and collapsed against the couch. With blurry vision, I stood up, placed my hands on either side of my hips, and loosed a deep breath.

"That was amazing." I breathed before straightening my back. I glanced over my shoulder at Damien, then back at Joshua, who was kneeling on the floor, bathed in yellow, florescent lighting. "You two are naturals."

Joshua snorted. "Not really."

"But you two enjoyed it, right?"

"Definitely."

"So, why don't I order us something to eat, and we can do it again? In a different position this time?"

Joshua stood up and offered me a small smile. "Okay."

Damien stood up and came to stand beside him. "I'm in."

I kissed one of them, then the other. "I'm really glad. I can't wait to feel both of you inside of me at the same time."

CHAPTER 6
THE ROYAL SCEPTER
TABITHA CHASE

She picked up the box and held it up to her face. "Why is this so heavy? What the hell did you order?"

Milo looked up from his phone, and his lips lifted into a smile. "I think it's finally here. I was beginning to think it was never going to come."

Ruby raised an eyebrow and set the box down on the coffee table. Milo stood up, set his phone down on the couch, and peered at the box intently. "What game did you order this time? Or this some kind of console?"

Milo shook his head, locks of chestnut hair moving back and forth. "It's not a console or a game. It's for the two of us."

Ruby placed both hands on her hips and frowned. "I already told you that couple games really aren't my thing. Sorry, babe. I know you want it to be."

Milo placed an arm around her shoulders and pulled her close. "It's not that kind of couple game."

Ruby stared up at his face. "What do you mean?"

"Do you remember the other night when I asked you what kind of role-playing fantasy you had?"

Ruby's eyes widened into saucers. She glanced down at the box then back up at her boyfriend's face. "What, really?"

Milo's grin stretched from ear to ear. "It took some searching, but I managed to find it." He removed his arm and opened the box. In the background, the TV blared, interrupted by the hissing of the tea kettle. Ruby ran into the kitchen and pulled the kettle away from the stove. Then, she poured the boiling hot water into two mugs and carried them back to the living room. Carefully, she set them down on the table before straightening her back.

He'd really done it.

On the couch, there were pieces of clothing already laid out, along with jewelry rings, a sword, a dagger, and two long cream-colored gloves. Slowly, Ruby reached out and fingered the material, the knots in her stomach tightening. Abruptly, she pulled her hand away and wiped it against the back of her jeans.

"Yeah, I don't think I can do this."

Milo spun around to face her, and his eyebrows drew together. "What do you mean? We talked about this. I even let you pick out the costumes."

"Yeah, but they look ridiculous. I'm never going to be able to take this seriously."

"You're not supposed to take it seriously." Milo wrapped both hands around my waist and tugged her against him. She tilted her head back to look up at his handsome face and kissed the smattering of stubble across his jaw. "It's supposed to be fun. At least try the clothes on. I'm sure you'll feel differently once you're in character."

Ruby's lips twitched. "You just want me to see me in whatever sexy outfit came."

Milo chuckled. "I do, but you didn't get a sexy outfit."

"Why not?"

Milo gestured behind him, to the simple brown dress draped over the side of the couch. Next to it, there was a sleeveless gray tunic, black leather boots, and a shift made of linen. Ruby drew away from him, walked over to the clothes, and held them up to the fluorescent lighting.

"I did want to be authentic." Ruby held the gown up to her body and smiled. "Okay, I guess I can grade those papers later."

Milo kissed the top of her head. "That's my girl. I mean milady."

Ruby burst into laughter. "I'm pretty sure that's not how you address me, but we can figure out the semantics lately."

Milo wrapped his arms around my waist and tugged me backward. "I can't wait, milady."

Milo went all out.

He stood in the middle of the dimly lit living room, with one hand on his hip and the other hanging by his side. He wore a well-embellished tunic with goldwork thread as a basic dress. On top of it, a surcoat was worn with an emblem symbolizing the king and his family. Finally, he wore a crimson robe on top, which glistened and rustled as he moved.

Ruby held his gaze and bowed her head. "Your Majesty."

Milo lifted his head up and cleared his throat. "Why have you asked for an audience with me?"

Ruby clasped her hands together and lowered her eyes to the floor. "I am sorry to bother you, Your Majesty, but I have come to beg."

"You wish to beg for what?"

"For my land back, Your Majesty." Ruby dropped to her knees, and the dress fluttered around her. "I am willing to do whatever Your Majesty deems necessary in order to gain favor."

"You wish to curry favor with the king?"

"Yes, Your Majesty."

Milo brushed past me and lowered himself onto the couch. He lifted his feet up and brought them to rest against the coffee table. "What can you have to offer me? You are nothing but a humble peasant woman."

Ruby rose to her feet and bit on the inside of her mouth. "I have nothing substantial to offer, Your Majesty. Perhaps you require a washing woman."

Don't laugh. You have to play the part, Ruby.

Suddenly, she lifted her gaze up, and Milo beckoned her forward. She stopped a few feet away and dipped into a curtesy. "Does this please Your Majesty?"

"I wish to see more of you before I decide."

"Your Majesty?"

"You must show me the state of your undergarments. How else am I expected to make such a decision?"

Ruby stood up straighter and smiled. "As you wish, Your Majesty."

With that, she pulled the top of the dress down. Then, with her eyes firmly locked on his face, she removed the dress and stood in her shift. A cold wind brushed past, so she shivered and wrapped her arms around herself.

"Come closer," Milo said in a clear voice. "I wish to see your handiwork more clearly."

Ruby stood directly in front of him and leaned forward, her breasts straining against the tight shift. Milo's eyes darted down, and his mouth darted out to lick his lips. Suddenly, he placed both hands on her hips and pulled her onto his lap. She shrieked, and her arms flailed at her sides.

"Your Majesty." Ruby giggled and batted her lashes at him. "We must not behave in such a manner. It is most inappropriate."

Milo's eyes moved over her face. "I am the king, and I can do whatever I please, and you are very pleasing, milady."

Ruby squirmed. "I am not a lady, Your Majesty. I am but a humble peasant girl."

Milo's hands came up around her neck, and her head spun. She leaned into the kiss and sighed. When he shifted against her, she wrenched her lips away and offered him a coy smile.

"What of my cleaning services, Your Majesty?"

"Huh?"

Ruby stood up and reached for Milo's trousers. Slowly, she pulled them down, her eyes never leaving his face. As soon as they were around his ankles, she pushed aside the robes, and her eyes went to the erection straining against his clear, white shift. The sight of his erection made the warmth in her belly grow hotter. Her legs tightened as she lowered herself onto the carpet. On her knees, she dipped her head so she was at eye level with his member and tilted her head back.

"I see that the royal scepter requires my attention."

Milo glanced down at her and blinked. "The royal scepter?"

"I shall be most attentive, Your Majesty." Ruby ran her hands along the shaft before she gripped him, hard. "You can trust me."

Milo released a harsh breath. "Oh, yes. I do believe you will do a fine job."

"I aim to please, Your Majesty." With that, she lifted up the shift and took him into her mouth. She sucked, slowly at first, then faster and faster until Milo wound his fingers through her hair. He tugged, and tears pricked the back of her eyes.

When he made a low growling noise, she smiled and drew back. "Am I not pleasing enough, Your Majesty?"

"You are not dressed appropriately, milady," Milo told her in a deep voice. "In order for me to determine if you would be well suited, you must undress."

Ruby placed a hand on her chest. "Oh, Your Majesty. I cannot. What would the people say?"

Abruptly, Milo stood up and yanked the shift down, allowing her breasts to spill forward. He cupped both of them in his hands and pressed them together. "They will say that you are a woman who is capable of pleasing her king."

Ruby's lips lifted into a half-smile. "You are too kind, Your Majesty."

Milo pressed his lips to her ear, his breath hot against the side of her neck. "And you are not wet enough, milady."

Ruby's stomach clenched. "I do not know what can be done, Your Majesty."

"Help me undress, and we shall see."

With fumbling fingers, they peeled the clothes off of him, leaving only a few rings on his fingers and the sword around his waist. Ruby pushed him onto the couch and climbed on top of him.

"You must allow me to show you a proper demonstration, Your Majesty."

Milo placed both hands on her waist and squeezed. "I am all yours, milady."

Ruby guided him into her and tossed her head back. "Oh, yes. Fuck."

"Am I pleasing to you, milady?"

"Your scepter is quite impressive, Your Majesty." Ruby squeezed her eyes shut and ground against him. "I am quite capable of tending to it."

Milo thrust upwards, and his grunt reverberated in her ears. "It will require much of your attention. Are you certain you are up to the task?"

Ruby forced one eye open and stared at him. "I shall certainly, Your Majesty."

"How attentive you are," Milo murmured, removing one hand and placing it on her breasts. "I can see how clean you are, milady."

He lowered his head and flicked one nipple, then the other. Milo took his time moving back and forth between the two while they rocked against each other, skin slapping against skin. Suddenly, Ruby arched her back and let out a deep, throaty groan.

"You must learn to temper your excitement, milady," Milo whispered into her neck. "Lest we be discovered."

"I shall be ruined if we are," Ruby mumbled, pausing to

place her hands on either side of his shoulders. "What are we to do?"

"We have time yet, milady," Milo replied. His mouth parted, and he nipped on her neck. "We must enjoy each other for as long as we can. Surely we should not deny each other such a pleasure."

When Milo began to rock side to side, Ruby squeezed her eyes shut and whimpered. She linked her fingers over his neck and thrust forward. His hands moved up and down her arms, leaving goosebumps everywhere he touched. When her orgasm ripped through her, leaving her gasping and panting, Milo stopped and leaned back.

"Why have you stopped, Your Majesty?"

Milo pushed her off and stood up. "You mock me, milady. You are not here to help me."

Ruby clasped her hands together. "I would never betray you, Your Majesty."

Milo frowned at her. "I saw your eyes wander, milady. You were planning on stealing my jewels."

Ruby buried her face in her hands and sniffed. "You must forgive me, Your Majesty. I would not have gone through with it."

Milo pulled her to her feet and pried her fingers away. "You intended to seduce me with your ample bosom and your generous figure, did you not?"

Ruby nodded.

Milo leaned forward and expelled a harsh breath. "I shall

have to punish you for such a crime then. It is a serious offense."

Ruby swallowed. "Of course, Your Majesty."

"Bend over," Milo instructed before lifting his chin up. He set the sword down on the floor and slid back into the crimson robes. "Did you not hear me? Kneel, woman."

Ruby's heart jumped into her throat. She spun around and bent down, so her face was pressed against the cushions. "How do you want me, Your Majesty?"

"You must place your legs on either side and hold absolutely still," Milo said.

After a brief pause, Ruby did as she was told, her pulse quickening when she felt him against her back. He dug his nails into her skin. "I will take what I want from you, and you will not protest. And you will speak of this to no one."

Ruby's heart thudded. "But Your Majesty—"

Milo slapped her ass, hard. "Silence. I did not give you permission to speak. I will have you, milady, and you will take all of me."

Ruby's stomach tightened. "Yes, Your Majesty."

Milo gave me another slap and grunted. In one swift move, he was inside of her. The couch dipped and creaked when he put one leg up. He thrust slowly at first, setting an even pace. As soon as she ground against him, he reached for her arms and twisted them behind her back.

"You will never disobey me," Milo whispered into her neck. "Do you understand me?"

"Yes, Your Majesty."

"Or I will have to punish you," Milo growled in a steady voice. "I take no pleasure in punishing my subjects, but you must be made to understand."

"I understand, Your Majesty. You must punish me further."

Milo's thrusts increased. "Have you learned your lesson?"

"Oh, yes." Ruby's head fell forward, and she pressed her lips together. "Harder, Your Majesty."

"My scepter is most pleased with your ministrations," Milo ground out, his breathing turning hot and heavy. "But I am afraid that it is not enough. I wish to gaze upon you while you are being punished."

"Wha—"

Before she could finish her question, Milo eased out and spun her around. He threw her over the back of the couch and rammed into her. Ruby cried out, and her arms came up around his back. She raked her nails over him and wrapped her legs over his waist. Milo's forehead was covered in a thin sheen of sweat, and the robes were clung to his flushed and sweaty skin, but he did not seem to care.

"You will look at me while I am punishing you," Milo ordered, pausing to cup her face in his hands. "You must not betray me again."

Ruby gasped. "I would never, Your Majesty."

Milo buried his face in her neck and circled his hips. Over

and over, he slammed into her, drawing out her pleasure and making the butterflies in her stomach erupt. As soon as they exploded, bringing her closer to the edge, she buried her face against his neck. Her tongue darted out, and she licked a path up to his earlobes and back again. Abruptly, he brought one hand up on either side of her and growled.

"You will never see another scepter again," Milo revealed, a hungry look in his eyes. "I wish to keep you all to myself."

Ruby pulled back and looked up at him. "It would be my pleasure to serve you, Your Majesty."

Milo left hot, open-mouthed kisses all over her neck, down the curve of her chest, and back up. As soon as his mouth closed on her eyes, his thrusts grew wilder and more frantic. So, she tightened her legs around his waist, and her hands traveled down to his ass. She gave it a firm and hard squeeze, earning a low, guttural noise from Milo. Then, he eased out, threw her legs up over his shoulders, and slammed back in, filling her all the way till the end.

Fuck.

Sharing her fantasy with him had been a good idea after all.

Eventually, sweat broke out across her back and down the sides of her face. A familiar sensation built up within her, and the fire in her veins turned molten. Suddenly, she threw her head back and cried out, repeating his name over and over until her spasms stopped. Once her chest stopped heaving, Milo eased out then slammed back into her. She placed a hand over his chest, on top of his heart, and felt it racing beneath her fingertips.

He was enjoying this as much as she was.

And there was something about having Milo on top of her, dressed in a robe with a royal insignia and rings on his fingers, that drove her crazy. She pressed her head against the side of his neck and left kisses there. Then, she made a low purring noise directly into his ear, causing Milo to curse.

"Fuck. You're making me so hard."

Ruby moaned. "You feel so good, Milo. Don't stop."

"I'm not going to stop. I want to keep fucking you."

"That's it. Mmm. Oh, yeah. Yeah, baby."

She exploded, spots dancing in her field of vision while she rode out her high. Shortly after, Milo's body jerked as he emptied himself into her. Then, he panted and rolled off of her onto the couch. The sounds of their heavy breathing filled the room, along with the smell of sweat and soap. Sometime later, Ruby ran a hand over her face and rubbed her eyes.

"Is His Majesty pleased?"

Milo chuckled and threw an arm around her. "Very, but I do believe we need to make a few adjustments."

Ruby patted his member and grinned. "Is the royal scepter not pleased?"

Milo tucked me into him, his chest rumbling with laughter. "Very pleased, but we have one more request."

Ruby tilted her head back and smiled up at him. "Anything you wish, Your Majesty."

"His Majesty wishes for a pizza with extra cheese and olives."

Ruby laughed and kissed him. "Whatever Your Majesty wishes."

CHAPTER 7

MRS. FERNANDEZ

BY CELIA STEVENS

"Mrs. Fernandez." Connor made a low choked noise and clasped both of my hands in his. I tilted my head back to look up at him, bathed in yellow florescent light, and frowned. "I don't think we should do this right now."

I raised an eyebrow. "Why not?"

"Maddie and Brayden are downstairs," Connor reminded me before casting a glance over his shoulder. "What if they come looking for me?"

"Didn't you tell them you need to make a phone call?" I tugged on the hem of his jeans, my fingers traveling up to the button and popping it open. Then I pulled the pants down and saw his erection straining against the fabric of his boxers.

"Yeah, but aren't they going to get suspicious?"

I stood up and pulled my shirt up over my head, my

breasts already eager to spill out of my bra. Then I reached behind and unhooked it. Connor's eyes went as wide as saucers, and the fabric of his boxers grew more taught.

Young men and their hormones.

Connor was barely twenty years old, but he already knew a lot about how to please a woman. In no small part, thanks to me. When my son befriended him, and he later took a liking to my daughter, it was almost too good to be true. I'd taken one look at his silky black hair, those dark almond-shaped eyes, and I knew I wanted him.

Luckily, he felt the same way.

"The two of them aren't going to notice if you're gone for fifteen or twenty minutes. Relax, Connor. You're worrying about this too much."

With that, I pulled his shirt up over his head, revealing defined muscles and a two-pack that I wanted to trace with my tongue. "Now, are we going to stand around and talk, or are you going to fuck me?"

Connor cleared his throat. "You know I want to, Missus Fernandez, but—"

"You try to rationalize this every time," I reminded him before pausing to shimmy out of my own jeans, allowing them to pool into a heap at my feet. "I don't care that you're friends with my kids. What we do with our own time is none of their business."

Connor's eyes roamed over me, and I knew his reluctance was wavering. "I want to."

I pressed a finger to his lips and smiled at him. "So, why aren't you? Why haven't you bent me over the bathroom sink already?"

Suddenly, I reached between his legs and cupped him over the fabric of his boxers. Connor made a low, choked noise and leaned into my touch. "Come on. You know you want to."

"Fuck."

In the next second, he was naked and riffling through his jeans for something. I crouched in front of him, took both of his hands in mine, and helped him get to his feet. "Sweetie, I'm on the pill. There's no need for that."

As soon as the words left my lips, he spun me around and began fondling my breasts. Then he bent me over the cold bathroom sink and stood behind me. In the full-length mirror, I saw him position himself and enter me in one long, measured stroke. My pulse quickened as his hands moved back and forth between my nipples, kneading and twisting until they were painfully hard. Afterwards, he kept one hand up, and the other darted underneath and sank in between my wet folds.

Connor wasted no time in finding my sweet spot.

Soon, there were two fingers, and it was all I could do not explode then and there. I really had taught him well, and I didn't care that the sound of skin slapping against skin was likely going to draw some attention. With my bedroom door locked and the TV volume pumped up, it was unlikely either of my kids was going to come banging on the door.

"You make so hard, Jenna." Connor breathed, his chest rising and falling unevenly. "I think about you all the time. You're so fucking hot."

"Mm." I rocked back and forth against him, enjoying the whimpering noises he was making. "Oh, God, yes. Connor. That's it. Right there. Fuck me harder."

Connor brought his head to rest against my back and thrust harder, faster. "Fuck. I could do this all day."

I twisted my arm over my head and gripped the back of his neck. "You should. We should fuck like this all the time."

Connor stopped, spun me around, and hoisted me up, so my legs were dangling off the bathroom sink. Bright afternoon light poured in through the window behind him, and I barely had time to register how cold the marble was against my bare ass before Connor threw one leg up over his shoulder and entered me again.

I gasped and threw my head back. "I see you've learned some new tricks."

Connor buried his face in my neck and continued to thrust. "I want to keep fucking you, Jenna."

My blood turned molten, and I raked my nails up and down his bare back. "Fuck, yes. Keep going. Don't stop."

Connor made a low growling noise and lowered his mouth to my breasts. He took one rosy nipple between his teeth and tugged before moving onto the other one. Meanwhile, his hands moved over every inch of my skin, leaving a trail of heat in his wake, and I felt young and alive, every nerve aware of him.

He smelled like soap and mint.

I wrapped my legs around his lower back and pulled him closer, our flushed chests pressed together. Connor said nothing, his mouth moving up to my neck, sucking and nipping on the skin there. Then he braced his hands on either side of the tile walls and circled his hips, the sound of skin slapping against skin reverberating inside of my head. My eyes squeezed shut, and I clenched around him, earning a choked gasp in return.

Suddenly, I was aware of the sound of my son's voice rising above the TV.

Connor lifted his head up, and his eyes met mine. "What if he finds us?"

"I don't care." I rocked my hips against his and linked my fingers over his neck. "He's a big boy. He'll be fine."

Connor groaned when I pressed my lips to his neck. "Fuck. I can't stop."

"Don't stop," I whispered, licking a path up to his ears. "Don't you dare stop until I'm screaming out your name, Connor."

He didn't respond, but he started thrusting with renewed vigor as if he was trying to drown out the sounds coming from outside. Soon, the two of us were rocking back and forth against each other with frenzied energy while I clawed at his back. When I began to chant his name, he placed a hand over my mouth and held my gaze. Again and again, he thrust into me until I fell over the edge, and he followed not long after. When he was done, he eased out of me and ran his fingers through his hair. I hopped off of the sink, wrapped my arms around his waist, and pressed a kiss to the back of his neck. Abruptly, Connor spun around and bent down to rummage through the clothes. When he picked up his jeans, he fished his phone out, his fingers flying over the keyboard. As soon as he was done, he reached for me and pulled me against him.

"I told them that I had to leave because of a work emergency." He nuzzled my neck, his hot breath sending shivers racing up and down my spine. "So, we've got some more time."

I linked my fingers over his neck and exhaled. "What did you have in mind?"

Connor drew himself away and took a step back. His eyes moved over every inch of me, studying me as I stood naked and glistening underneath the harsh, white light. By the time he was done, goosebumps had broken out across my flesh, and I was wet.

Again.

Damn, I loved young men and their stamina.

He could keep going all night, and I wanted to let him.

Suddenly, his phone buzzed, interrupting the moment. Connor muttered something under his breath and reached for it. His entire face changed when he looked down and typed up a quick response. As soon as he was done, he crossed over to me and kissed me. I arched my back and melted against him.

"They're both going out," Connor murmured against my lips. "They won't be back for hours."

I peeled myself off of him, took his hand, and led him into the bedroom. "In that case, we should definitely use the bed."

Connor's mouth found the back of my neck, and he sucked on the sensitive skin there. "I want to fuck you everywhere."

I spun around to face him. "Everywhere?"

Connor twisted my arms behind my back and held them in place. "Everywhere. I want to fuck you on the bed, against the windows, on the dresser, in the shower...."

"It's a good thing we have a few hours then."

Connor smirked and lifted my arms up over my head. Suddenly, he reached for my legs and hoisted me up. I wrapped my legs around him as he moved us backward, and we fell onto the bed. Immediately, his mouth began to move over the rest of my life, kissing a path straight down to my navel. Slowly, he looked up at me, his eyes wide and searing. Connor lowered himself so he was at eye level with my center and kissed the inside of my thighs.

My heart jumped into my throat. "Fuck."

"We're just getting started," Connor promised in a low

and husky voice. His lips found their way to my center, and he used two fingers to push into my wet folds. Then, his mouth came on top of me and licked.

I arched my back and squeezed my eyes shut. "Shit. Connor that feels so good."

He flicked his tongue back and forth, nails digging into my waist. Then, he moved up and down, pausing to blow hot air against my center. Warmth pooled in the center of my stomach, and my muscles tightened. I wound my fingers through his hair and tried to hear past the pounding of my own heart.

All too quickly, my orgasm came, ripping through me and leaving me breathless. When I climbed down from my high, and my vision cleared, Connor pulled me up to my feet. He led me over to the window, overlooking the street and the garden, and bent me over.

"No one can see us," I assured him in a deep and husky voice. "I made sure that the windows are anti-reflection."

Connor kissed the back of my neck and grunted. "Good."

With that, he eased himself into me. He held himself still while my muscles expanded. As soon as they did, I ground against him, and he released a deep breath. Connor placed his hands on either side of the cool glass and thrust forward, earning a deep moan. Then, he eased back out and back in, harder this time. Before long, the two of us were grinding against each other, moving back and forth while sweat dripped down my back and the sides of my face. My vision was unfocused and hazy as I looked out onto the street below, barely making out the cars that drove past.

Connor twisted my arms over my back. "Do you want me to go harder?"

"Yes."

Connor released my arms, and his pace increased. "Fuck. You make me so hard, Jenna. All I can think about is fucking you. All the damn time."

"I don't want you to stop." I groaned, squeezing my eyes shut. "Fuck, yes, Connor. Just like that."

Connor's breathing grew sharp. "You're so tight, and you're so sexy."

Another orgasm ripped through me, abrupt and leaving me breathless. I stood up and sucked in huge mouthfuls of air. When my chest was no longer tight, I walked past Connor and over to the dresser. I hopped onto it, spread my legs open, and beckoned him forward. In an instant, Connor was in front of me again, this time with both of my legs thrown over his shoulders.

"Don't close your eyes this time," Connor told me in a thick voice. "I want you to watch me while I fuck you."

In one quick thrust, he was inside of me again. This time, he moved from side to side while I raked my fingers over his back. He hissed and buried his head against my neck. I threw my head back and scooched closer to the edge of the dresser. He kept one hand on the mirror, and the other dug into my hips, leaving crescent-shaped marks.

The dresser began to creak and groan under our weight.

Soon, the smell of Connor's sweat and soap filled the room. I closed my eyes and inhaled. When Connor stopped, I wrapped my legs around him, and my eyes flew open. "Keep fucking me."

Connor's eyes darkened. "I love how bossy you are. You're so fucking sexy."

I drew him closer and brought my head to rest against his shoulder. In the mirror on top of the bed, I saw the two of us rocking back and forth against each other, and my pulse quickened. Connor's arms reached between us, pressing my breasts together, and a jolt of electricity ripped through me.

Shit.

He sure had been doing his homework.

Every touch and every kiss moved through me, leaving fire in its wake. Eventually, I unhooked my legs and tilted my head towards the bed. Connor eased out of me and carried me to the bed. I crawled up on my hands and knees and waited. In the mirror, I saw him position himself from behind and the feral look on his face when he glanced into the mirror.

"Look at us fucking," Connor growled into my back. "We should do this all the time."

Over and over, he slammed into me, skin slapping against skin. When my arms grew tired, I leaned forward and brought my elbows to rest against the mattress. Connor placed his hands on either side of my hips and kept me in place, his motions growing faster and more frenzied. When his breathing grew sharp, and he jerked, I thrust backward into him. Then, my own release came, just as I felt his warmth seep in between my legs. I gasped, my vision dancing in and out of focus. Slowly, Connor eased himself out of me and collapsed into the mattress. Slowly, I lowered myself onto my stomach and spread my arms out on either side of me.

I forced one eye open and saw Connor staring at me. "What?"

Connor tucked a lock of hair behind my ear. "You're the most beautiful woman I've ever seen."

I snorted and sat up straighter. "Oh, please."

Connor nodded. "It's true. I'm not just saying that because we're fucking."

I ran a hand over my face and pushed myself up onto my elbows. "Connor, this doesn't need to be something it's not, okay? We both know what that this is."

Connor's lips lifted into a smile. "Oh, yeah? What's that?"

"You and me having a good time." I threw one leg over him, then the other, so I was straddling him. Connor's eyes widened when I pressed my breasts against his chest and leaned forward. "I like fucking you, and you like fucking me. We're good together."

Connor's fingers splayed over my back. "Just good?"

"We're great together," I amended, lowering my head for

a kiss. When he responded, I drew back and ground against him. Connor groaned and threw his head back. "I want to keep fucking you."

Connor's arm circled my waist. "I want to keep doing that too."

"Good, so less talking and more fucking."

Later, when we finished, I tied a robe around my waist and hurried down the stairs. Connor peered out the back door then spun around to kiss me. My toes curled, and my head spun when he did. He drew back and offered me a bright smile. I placed both hands on my hips and offered him a smirk.

"Come back tonight. I'll let you in through the back door."

CHAPTER 8

MISSIONARY IMPOSSIBLE

BY KELLY JAX

"Don't worry," Mateo assured me before he bent down and flicked the lighter on. A yellow flame came to life and danced in front of him, illuminating his features before he moved it away. Then the candle came to life, and the scent of vanilla and berries filled the room. In the background, soft jazz music wafted through the speakers.

I clasped my hands behind my back and swallowed. "Okay."

Mateo stood up and spun around to face me. "You don't need to sound like you're walking the plank."

I chuckled nervously. "I'm not. Sorry, I'm just nervous."

Mateo pocketed his lighter and strolled towards me. He stopped when he was a breadth away and took my hands in his. I tilted my head back to look at him, saw the warmth in his crystal blue eyes, and my stomach dipped.

I wanted this.

More than anything.

So, there was no reason to be nervous.

Mateo and I had known each other for most of our lives, having spent a decade being friends and running around the block wreaking havoc. After years of skinned knees, rolling around in the mud, and playing pranks on each other, we'd kissed underneath a streetlamp on a warm spring day.

Now, here we were years later, in my college dorm, about to have sex for the first time. Although I'd spent many nights tossing and turning and wondering about it, I knew experiencing it for the first time was going to be different. No amount of reading books or online research was going to prepare me for the real thing.

Mateo lifted my hands up to his lips and pressed a soft kiss to them. "You have nothing to be nervous about. We don't have to do this if you don't want to."

I cleared my throat. "I want to. I just don't know what to do."

"Relax," Mateo offered with a bright smile. "And follow my lead."

"You're so bossy."

"Oh, please. You love it." Mateo tugged on my hands and pulled me into his arms. He placed both hands on the small of my waist, leaned in, and kissed me. As soon as his lips met mine, stars exploded behind my eyelids, and my entire body came alive. When my heart began to pound in my ears, I sighed and leaned into him. Mateo nipped on my lower lip, and when my lips parted, we began a sensual battle for dominance.

He maneuvered us backwards until my knees hit the edge of the bed, and I fell. Slowly, he drew away and pulled his shirt up over his head. I ran my hands along Mateo's warm chest and stopped at the smattering of dark chest hair. Then I pressed my lips to his skin and licked. He linked his fingers over my head and exhaled deeply.

"You make me feel so good, Aly."

"I do?"

"Always," Mateo murmured in a deep voice. "And I'm going to make you feel good, I promise. It's going to hurt for a bit, then it'll be okay."

I leaned back to look up at him. "I trust you."

"I'll go slow," Mateo promised, before kissing me again, deeper this time. When I began to lean back against the mattress, Mateo climbed onto the bed, and it creaked and groaned beneath him. As soon as I lowered my back onto the bed, Mateo pulled away and undid each shirt button, taking his time with each one until it felt like I was on fire. Out of the corner of my eye, I saw the night lamp flicker, casting long yellow shadows across the wall before it stilled. Mateo loomed over me, placed one hand on the headboard, and used his other hand to frame my face in his hands.

Suddenly, his other hand was moving up and down my arms, leaving a trail of tingles in their wake. It wasn't long before my entire skin broke out into goosebumps, and a familiar tightening began in between my legs. Mateo smiled and pressed his lips to my neck, leaving hot, open-mouthed kisses there. He kissed a path up to my ears and tugged on one lobe, then the other. Meanwhile, his hands moved to my back, making quick work of undoing my bra. As soon as he unhooked it, he bent down and took a nipple between his teeth.

I arched my back and moaned. "Oh, God. That feels so good."

Mateo moved to the other nipple and looked up at me. "I can't wait to be inside you, Aly."

I swallowed and gave him a small smile. "Me neither."

Slowly, he leaned back on his legs and began to undress me, tossing my skirt over his shoulder. Once he was done, he fumbled with his own jeans before they joined the pile of clothes on the floor. Mateo's eyes moved over, taking every inch of skin and every freckle until he stopped at my face. With a gentle look, he leaned forward and kissed me. I sighed and leaned into the kiss, fire coursing through my body. When he nipped on my lower lip, I granted him entrance, and his tongue darted into my mouth, beginning a sensual battle for dominance.

He tasted like chocolate and beer.

I wanted to lose myself in him.

So, I arched my back and sat up, pressing myself closer. Mateo smiled into the kiss and wrapped his arms around me.

He kept one arm on the small of my back while the other traced a path down the slope of my back and back up to my shoulders. Then, he began to knead the muscles there, earning a deep and throaty moan. Little by little, he began to pull away until we were looking at each other. Wordlessly, he pulled on my legs, so I was flat on my back.

Mateo lowered himself onto the mattress and pressed his mouth against the inside of my thigh. "We're got all night. I'm not in a hurry. I want you to enjoy your first time."

I released a deep breath, some of the knots in my stomach loosening. "Okay."

Mateo shifted and adjusted his legs underneath him. "Relax, baby. It's going to be okay."

With that, he placed his arms on either side of me, and his kissing grew more sensual. He ran his mouth along the inside of my thighs, stopping inches away from the center. Then, he switched to the other thigh and did the same, leaving a trail of heat in his wake. The knots in my stomach turned into butterflies, and sweat formed on the back of my neck.

"Mateo."

"I know," Mateo whispered against my skin. "I know you want me to be inside of you. We'll get there."

His mouth stopped in front of my clit, and his tongue darted out to lick. Fire exploded within me, and I lifted my hips up off the mattress. Mateo pushed his tongue into my wet folds and licked, hard.

A gasp fell from my lips. "Shit, you feel so good, Mateo."

"I'm just getting started." Mateo gripped either side of my thighs and held me in place. "Tell me how fast you want me to go."

He glanced up at me, and his lips lifted into a smile. "You're so fucking sexy right now."

My heart hammered against my chest. "Look who's talking."

Mateo smiled and switched his gaze back to my center. He buried his face in between my thighs, and his mouth disappeared into my mound. Of their own accord, my hands came up over his neck and fisted themselves through his hair. His tongue moved slowly, lazily, as if we had all the time in the world. I squirmed, and he delved further, until he found my sweet spot.

I cried out his name, and his pacing changed.

Mateo released my thighs and pressed his hands against the mattress. He muttered something, but I couldn't hear him, not when I was lost in a thick haze. So, I lifted my hips up and ground against him, needing to feel him.

When I felt a rumble against my center, my lips stretched into a grin. "Oh, baby. Oh, that feels so good. Don't stop."

His fingers dig into either side of my hips, teasing the sensitive flesh there. I glanced down at the top of his head, and my pulse quickened. Suddenly, Mateo looked up at me through hooded eyes, and another wave of heat moved directly to my core. He wrenched his gaze away and returned to my center, his tongue moving back and forth then up and down.

Each swipe drove me closer and closer to the edge.

Abruptly, I released his hair, and my hands fell on either side of me. They gripped the sheets, and my eyes squeezed shut. Spots danced behind my eyelids, and the tightening in my stomach only grew. One of Mateo's arms traveled up until it came to a rest on top of my breasts. He squeezed and pressed them together.

Meanwhile, his other hand moved to my navel, pressing down. I twisted my head to the side and moaned, another wave of desire, stronger this time, washing over me. When I did come, Mateo waited until I stopped shaking and writhing before he removed his mouth. He crawled forward and pressed his lips to mine, making me taste my own juices.

It was saltier than I expected.

And the look on his face sent more heat rushing to my nether regions. Wordlessly, Mateo settled next to me, and his fingers caressed my skin. By the time I caught my breath and my vision cleared again, his hand was already on my center. He stroked me and knelt down to press a kiss to my lips. As soon as I moved to deepen the kiss, he pushed one finger and another.

I made a low choking noise in the back of my throat.

Mateo swiped back and forth, then up and down. Suddenly, he wrenched his lips away, and his mouth moved to my neck. He pressed hot, open-mouthed kisses there until he reached my earlobes. Slowly, he tugged on one then the other until I was panting and squirming against him. I felt his eyes on me as he lowered his mouth to my breasts and took one nipple between his teeth.

When his mouth closed around it, my muscles clenched around his fingers. He moved his mouth to the other nipple and did the same, only harder. I arched my back and tossed my head to the side. My hands moved to his shoulders, and I dug my nails there. Later, I realized I was calling out his name and muttering unintelligibly. As soon as I blinked, I saw Mateo hovering over me, a smile etched onto his face.

"Do you feel more relaxed now?"

I nodded. "I want you, Mateo."

He bent down to kiss me. "I want you too. So fucking much."

He held himself still and stared down at me. Then, he stood up and walked over to the nightstand. As soon as I saw the condom, I stretched and curled my legs up in front of me. Mateo lowered his knees onto the bed, leaned forward, and positioned himself at my entrance. His eyes never left my face as he ripped the condom open with his teeth and rolled it onto his erection.

"Tell me if you want me to stop or slow down." A thin sheen of sweat broke out over his forehead. He waited for me to nod before he pushed himself in and waited. I tensed and breathed out through my mouth, disliking the stinging sensation. Still, I focused on my breathing and the sound of Mateo's reassuring whispers.

When the stinging subsided, he eased out and back in, slower this time. I linked my feet together over his ass and held him still. Mateo stopped, looked down at me, and pressed a kiss to my forehead. Then I wriggled against him, and he began to increase his pace. I lifted my hands up and ran them along the length of his back, down to his ass and back up.

He was so big, yet somehow he filled every inch of me.

Mateo bent down and kissed me. "You feel so good, Aly. You're so tight."

"You feel so...big."

Mateo chuckled. "I'm glad you like it."

I tilted my head back and studied his face. "I do."

Mateo threw his head back and groaned. "God, you're so sexy, Aly. And so wet and warm."

I made a low whimpering noise and squeezed my eyes shut. "I—*Oh, yes*."

Mateo pushed himself in further and placed his hands on either side of me. "You like that, huh? How about this?" He eased out and back into me. "Does that feel good?"

I released a deep breath. "Mmm, yeah, it does."

Little by little, the discomfort began to wear off, and he began to feel better inside of me like he was meant to be there. Eventually, I began to move against him, meeting each thrust with one of my own until a familiar tightening began in the pit of my stomach. Then my heart started to pound in my ears, and my lungs burned. When I did come, it was with a deep moan that reverberated inside of my head. My body writhed and spasmed against his, and my fingers curled at my sides, bunching up the sheets underneath me. Mateo pressed his forehead to mine, and his thrusting slowed and stopped altogether. By the time my vision cleared, Mateo was holding himself very still, the sweat on his forehead glistening.

"How was it?"

I reached up to kiss him. When I pulled back, I brushed his hair out of his eyes. "You don't have to stop."

Mateo released a deep breath. "Are you sure?"

"I like feeling you inside of me," I whispered, bringing my forehead to rest against his. "I want you to keep going, Mateo. Please."

Mateo made a low choked noise. Then, he moved again, easing in and out in long and practiced strokes. I linked my fingers together over his head and kept my legs slightly curled over me. He buried his head in the crook of my neck and sighed, the smell of soap washing over me. I squeezed my eyes shut and relaxed my legs. When Mateo's thrusts changed, growing more urgent and pronounced, my stomach clenched. I wrapped my legs around his waist and shifted, pressing a kiss to the side of his head. Mateo twisted his head to the side and captured his lips with mine.

His kiss made my head spin.

When he pulled back, I inhaled, and he slammed into me. I gasped and made a strange choking noise. Then, Mateo eased out and slammed back into me with a little more force than necessary. He leaned back and glanced down at my face.

"Do you want me to go slow?"

I shook my head. "No, I like this. Keep going."

"Are you sure?"

"Mateo, I want you to keep doing exactly what you're doing," I told him, struggling to hear past the pounding in my ears. "Don't make me beg."

Mateo smirked. "I like it when you beg."

With that, he brought his forehead to rest against mine and settled into a rhythm. Every now and again, I lifted my hips up off the mattress and ground into him, enjoying the sounds of his grunts and groans. I ran my hands along the length of his back, paused at his ass, and squeezed. Mateo growled and lifted my arms up over my head. He held them in a vice-like grip while the other hand touched and teased every inch of skin, leaving me gasping for more. Eventually, he released my arms and braced himself on either side of me. Sweat formed on the back of his neck and fell in rivulets down his back.

I reached up and licked the side of his face, and his answering grunt made me pulse quicken. Then, I fell backwards against the mattress, squeezed my legs tighter around him, and groaned. Mateo's mouth moved against my neck, sucking and biting while he continued to thrust in and out. Suddenly, he went still before he began to writhe and spasm on top of me. His entire body jerked, and I felt warmth pool in between my legs. Mateo gasped and squeezed his eyes shut. Then, he eased out of me and collapsed onto the mattress next to me.

Later, when I could breathe again, I curled up to him, and he tucked me into his side. "I could definitely get used to this."

Mateo laughed and pressed a kiss to the side of my head. "Good, because we're just getting started."

CHAPTER 9

THE CIGAR CLUB

BY JEFF DIAZ

She placed one hand on her hip and raised an eyebrow. "I didn't know you boys were such horny fuckers?"

I glanced back at his friends, Jack and Bryan, who nodded lustfully. The three of us exchanged a quick look before I stood up to face the blonde woman who stood in front of me. She straightened her back, and her hands eased down the front of her skirt to smooth it out. Then, she held my gaze, and a slow smile spread across her face.

In the dim lighting of the hole-in-the-wall New York City cigar club, she was the most beautiful thing I'd ever seen. With flecks of gold in her hazel eyes and a body I'd been fantasizing about for the past few months, I could hardly believe she was standing there. Much less that we'd convinced her to give all three of us a chance.

Maybe my therapist was right.

None of this had to be uncomfortable or bottled up.

Not when all four of us were willing and ready.

You see, us boys had been coming to this cigar club for a monthly boys' night for a while now. We smoke and drink whiskey and fantasize about our favorite cocktail waitress. Tonight, however, we got bold and told her about our fantasy. Her response? "We close at 1am. Stick around until then... and there's an ATM out front."

So, a few hours later, I reached into my pocket and pulled out some crisp folded bills. Wendy took them from me, and my smile grew wider. She tucked the money into her pocket and flipped her hair over her shoulder. Abruptly, she walked off and stopped in front of the mahogany counter. The chandelier above her flickered, and the din of conversation reverberated inside of my head. Getting fuckin' excited, I stood up straighter and glanced around at the deserted brown leather booths and squinted through the smoke that hung in the air around me.

Money talks in New York

And you can get anything you want.

With that thought in mind, I wheeled around and found Wendy hurrying towards us. Jack and Bryan came to stand on either side of me, wearing identical impatient and hungry expressions. Wendy took my hand in hers and led us down a narrow hallway and through a door in the back. She paused to give us all a smile before leading us up a flight of stairs. At the top, she stopped and pushed the door open.

Wendy released my hand and stepped in. "Come on in."

White light flickered on, and I involuntarily winced. I studied the sparsely furnished apartment, from the mismatched living room set facing the old TV to the frayed carpet beneath my feet. When Wendy spread my arms out on either side of her, I gave her a slow smile.

"Nice place."

"You don't have to do that," Wendy told me. "I don't need you to compliment my place when we both know it's shit, but at least it's right above where I work, and I can afford it."

I nodded. "Okay."

Wendy took off her vest and began to unbutton her shirt. "So, how are we going to do this?"

Jack took a step forward, and his eyes moved over her, slowly. "Whatever you want."

Wendy glanced over at Bryan. "How about you, big guy? You got any ideas?"

Bryan covered the distance between them and kissed her. Wendy drew back after a while and grinned. "Okay, this is going to be fun."

I could tell she was telling the truth.

Suddenly, she spun around and bent down. She let her skirt fall to a puddle beneath her feet, followed by her shirt. As soon as she was left in her black lace panties and bra, she spun around to face us. Her tongue darted out to lick her dry lips. Wordlessly, I walked over to her and kissed her. She moaned into my mouth, and her hands came up around my neck.

Wendy pulled back and gave Jack a sultry smile. "The others are on their way." She had told us she likes an audience. Fuckin' fine by me.

Shortly after, a man and a woman knocked on Wendy's door. Jack opened the door for them, and they hurried inside, a flurry of flushed activity. Deftly, they pulled out two chairs and dragged them to the kitchen counter, overlooking the living room. Wendy gave them a thumbs up before returning her attention to Jason.

Fuck. An entourage. She'd done this before. A real professional.

Abruptly, Wendy pulled back and removed her last article of clothing, leaving her completely naked. She gestured to Jack and Bryan, who did the same. "This is Ben, and this is Penny. Ben is my bodyguard. Penny is my apprentice, a fluffer." Wendy laughed.

Both of them waved.

Us boys looked at each other. I guess this is how it's done in New York City.

Wendy reached for me, and with sure and steady movements, she helped me out of my clothes. As soon as she did, she claimed my mouth with hers, and her tongue slid in, beginning a sensual battle for dominance. All of the blood rushed to my dick, and it took everything within me not to bend her over and take her right then and there. As if she sensed my train of thought, Wendy pulled back and walked over to the others. Out of the corner of my eye, I saw her bend down in front of Bryan to stroke him. Then, she took him in her mouth, and fuck, did he start to groan.

Penny, the fluffer, stepped forward in a red thong and a bra that strained against her skin. She pointed at Jack, and he came to a stand next to me.

Penny's gaze switched back and forth between us two while she lowered herself to the floor. She kissed my cock, and gripped Jack's. In the back of her throat, Penny made low whimpering noises while she alternated between us, offering an unobstructed view of Wendy on her hands and knees in front of Bryan. Bryan threw his head back and pushed himself further into her mouth.

Wendy made a low whimpering noise that made me even harder.

I glanced down at the top of Penny's head wound my fingers around the back of her neck. She took me in her and sucked, sending wave after wave of pleasure washing over me. Meanwhile, she kept one hand on my thigh and the other on Jack, her nimble fingers moving up and down until Jack groaned and sweat broke out across his forehead.

The knots in my stomach tightened.

Penny withdrew and tilted her head back to look at me. "You're good to go, sexy."

I offered her a smile. Then, I walked over to Wendy and Bryan, who were standing in the middle of the living room.

Penny and Jack came to stand next to us, forming a circle. Quickly, Wendy eased back and sat on her heels. She gave Bryan a bright smile, and he smirked. Penny glanced up at him, and the two of them exchanged a quick, lustful look. I took a step forward then another until I was standing in front of Wendy. I helped her up to her feet and kissed her. When she was breathless, she pulled back and took both of me hands. After placing them on her hips, she reached between them and stroked me.

I growled; I couldn't help myself.

Her lips lifted into a smile as she stopped. She turned around and bent down, offering herself up to me. I positioned myself at her back, and in one quick thrust, I was inside of her. Over and over, the two of us rocked back and forth against each other, with Wendy's cries of pleasure filling the room. I dug my fingers into her hips and squeezed my eyes shut.

Fucking hell.

She was so tight.

Soon, the smell of her sweat and soap was all I could smell. Then, she was calling out my name and panting for breath. Her body shook as she felt her orgasm rip through her, and rivulets of sweat slid down her back. I kissed her back, and my tongue darted out to lick her flushed skin. Wordlessly, Wendy eased off of me and spun around to face me. She gave me a quick peck on the lips before reaching for Jack. (What a fucking pro.) Jack allowed her to pull her to him, and his hands immediately went to her ass.

I took a few steps back, and Penny's hand immediately found my dick. She stroked me while sucking on Bryan, moving quickly and deftly, her low whimpers making my blood boil.

I cocked his head to the side and watched as Wendy led Jack to the couch. He sat down and smiled up at her. She threw one leg on either side of him and lowered herself onto him. In one quick movement, Bryan was inside of her, and the two of them ground against each other with reckless abandon.

I could not look away.

By the time Wendy came for me, my cock was pulsing and twitching, and I was ready to bury myself deep inside of her. Her eyes were hooded and full of a feral hunger I recognized. So, she took me to the couch and lowered her pussy onto my face. My heart pounded as I kissed the inside of her thighs. When I reached her center, I placed my mouth there and got to fuckin' work.

Wendy bucked against me and made a low, unintelligible noise.

I thrust myself in between her legs and placed my hands on either side of her. I kissed and sucked on her wet cunt, and inhaled, the taste of her juices making my insides tighten. She gripped the back of my neck and thrust upwards, driving me further inside. I squeezed my eyes shut and listened to the sound of her voice, allowing it to guide him.

Holy shit, she was sexy.

And there was nothing I liked more than a woman who knew what she wanted.

It was a good thing she wanted several men at the same time.

Fuck.

I flicked my tongue back and forth, then I moved up and down, wanting as much of her as he could get. When she writhed and spasmed on top of me, I leaned back and crawled up. Firmly, she placed a kiss on my mouth, and with an impish smile, she walked over to her counter.

She opened the lid of a small, but beautiful cigar humidor. She pulled out an unbanded cigar, and lifted it up to her nose to smell. "This is the new blend, it's unreal."

In a few seconds, she had clipped the cigar, and placed it in her mouth. She pulled out a torch-style lighter, and fired up the stick. She looked at me through the smoke, and my already ready hard cock grew even a little bit more. I'd never seen Wendy smoke a cigar, and fuck, did she look good.

She approached, her cigar now burning bright. She took a puff, then held the cigar in her hand and passed it to me. "You should smoke this while you fuck me."

I hadn't even told her that was part of my fantasy, but she just knew somehow. Fuck, she knows what men like.

She positioned herself on the couch on her back and

shimmied that hot cunt down. I got on my knees, cigar in my mouth and sat back on my heels. I held the cigar in my jaw, and took a few puffs while I explored her pussy with my fingers.

As the room filled with smoke, I leaned forward and thrust into her.

Wendy threw her head back and moaned.

The two of us moved in sync, rocking back and forth against each other. Our grunts and moans seemed to hang in the air with the smoke. I reached for her tits and felt her hard nipples. Little bits of cigar ash fell on her stomach, but she didn't mind. In fact, I could tell she liked it.

"That's it, Wendy. That's a good girl. You want more, don't you?" I moved my hand down her body, and using my thumb, I went after her clit - a move many women have praised me for in the past. I wanted Wendy to enjoy this as mush as I was. She looked me dead in the eye. I could tell she was close. Through the cigar held in my teeth, I said, "Cum for me, baby."

Suddenly, Wendy was orgasming again, only this time her chest was heaving. He body was shaking involuntarily and fuck did she moan. When her breathing evened out, my own orgasm came, and my entire body shook with tremors. I came inside her in several quick thrusts, and held my cock deep in her for a few seconds before easing out. As soon as I stood up, Jack came to stand in front of Wendy, and the two of them exchanged a quick look before he knelt down in front of her. He threw both of her legs over his shoulders and thrust in. He had a cigar in his jaw too; I must have missed him lighting up while I was fucking her.

Wendy's eyes squeezed shut.

She rocked back and forth against Jack, making low whimpering noises as she did. I took a step back, and underneath the dim lighting, I watched, my still-hard cock twitching at the sight. Although I'd already completely emptied himself in her, it wouldn't be long before I felt ready to go again. So, I walked over to the counter, where Ben had laid out an assortment of snacks and drinks. Wordlessly, I emptied two bottles of water and ripped through two snack bars.

When I turned back around, Wendy was draped over the side of the couch, and Jack was still moving. (Although it was getting hard to see all this through the smoke in the room.)

Penny was standing behind Bryan, both of her legs wrapped around him, and her breasts pressed against his back. She reached around him to light his cigar.

My eyes swept over the room before I rejoined the fun. Fuck, this night was just beginning.

I'd never be able to smoke a cigar again without getting rock hard.

CHAPTER 10

HOTTER THAN HELL

BY JANE CARMICHAEL

"Gabriel's perfect," I whispered into my husband's ear. Eric twisted to face me, his dark eyes full of mischief. "And I'm pretty sure he'd be into it. I've been dropping hints for a while."

Eric raised a dark eyebrow. "You didn't waste any time at all."

I leaned in and pressed a kiss to the side of his neck. "Because I love experiencing this with you."

Eric pushed my hair back, and his hand traveled further up my thigh. "I can't wait to watch someone else fucking you."

Desire rushed straight to my stomach, and then a little lower.

I sat up straight and scanned the room for him, finding him instantly. He was dressed in a pair of dark trousers, a button-down shirt, and an easy smile on his face. When he realized I was looking up at him, he excused himself, brushing past rows of other partygoers, and came to a stop right in front of us.

Hot damn, he was sexy.

And I couldn't wait to have his hands all over me while Eric watched.

I was turned on just thinking about it.

Gabriel's lips lifted into a smile. He pulled out a chair and lowered himself onto it. After he signaled for a drink, he twisted to face us with a bright smile. "So, when are we going to leave?"

Eric's grip on my thigh tightened. "We should stay for a few more minutes since it is a work event."

Gabriel politely shrugged. "Whatever you want."

"Did Lucy explain everything to you?" Eric reached for his glass of water and took a few quick sips. "Is there anything you want to go over?"

Gabriel shook his head and took a sip of his drink. "No, it's all good."

I glanced between the two of them before reaching into my own drink. Then, I downed it all in one gulp, the liquid burning a path down my throat before it settled in the pit of my stomach. The warmth spread throughout my limbs and down to the tips of my toes. An hour later, I was giggling, the warmth in my stomach still bubbling as we left the building. Eric had his arm on the small of my back as he steered me towards the car. As soon as I got in, I twisted around to watch the two of them exchange a few quick words before joining me in the car.

Eric started the engine, and we drove off.

When we arrived at our apartment, I took the stairs two at a time. I was panting and breathless as Eric inserted the key into the lock. Inside, I fumbled for the switch and winced when the yellow lighting came on. Then, I spun around and kicked off my shoes. Gabriel kicked the door shut with the back of his leg and glanced around, his eyes lingering on the French doors, leading out onto a balcony overlooking the glittering city.

"Like what you see?"

Gabriel's eyes snapped to attention, and he stood up straighter. "I'd like it even better if you were naked."

Color rushed to my cheeks. I undressed with trembling fingers, leaving myself in my bra and panties. Gabriel's eyes widened, and he shoved his hands into his pockets. I cast a quick glance in Eric's direction. His tie was already askew, and his hair was messy atop his head. He held a glass of whiskey in his hands, and impatience played out across his features before he stamped it out.

You've done this before, Lucy. No need to get nervous.

With a flick of my hair, I walked over to Gabriel and palmed him over his trousers. His lips parted, and his eyes widened into saucers. "Are you going to stand there all day, or are you going to do something?"

Gabriel nodded, and his hands moved to my ass.

When he claimed his lips with mine, my blood turned molten. While I angled my head to deepen the kiss, my fingers moved up to his chest. I flicked one button and then the next until I was done. Then, I pushed his shirt up over his shoulders, and it fluttered to the floor. When I was done, I wrenched my lips away and breathless, and with my stomach twisting into tight knots, I reached for his belt buckle.

Gabriel captured both of my hands in his and shook his head. "I'll do it."

I nodded, and my throat turned dry. Eric brushed past us and dimmed the lights, casting the room in a soft and warm glow. Then, my husband walked back to the counter, pulled out a chair, and sat down. His eyes were wide and watchful when Gabriel kissed me again. This time, he nipped on my lower lip until I granted him access. His tongue darted in, tasting like whiskey and mouthwash. I arched my back and melted against him, shivers breaking out across my body when his hands moved up and down.

Abruptly, Gabriel stopped, took my hand, and led me to the couch. He looked over at Eric, and there was a strange glint in his eyes. "What do you want me to do?"

Eric took a sip and cleared his throat. "Lick her pussy."

I threw Eric a smile over my shoulder before lowering myself onto the couch. Wordlessly, Gabriel knelt down onto the carpet and buried himself in between my legs. His mouth was hot and demanding against my skin. He pressed hot, open-mouthed kisses until he reached my center. Then, his nails dug into the skin on either side of my hips, and his tongue darted in between my wet folds.

My hips rose of their own accord, and I moaned.

Gabriel's tongue flicked back and forth, venturing in until he found my sweet spot. When he did, his tongue darted lazily, licking a path up before moving down. Now and again, he stopped and blew on my center, sending shivers racing up and down my spine. My fingers came up around his neck and threaded themselves through his hair.

Holy shit.

Clearly, this wasn't Gabriel's first rodeo.

When my stomach began to tighten into knots, and a familiar sensation bubbled within me, I threw my head back. I squeezed my eyes shut, and my pulse quickened. Abruptly, I spasmed and writhed, the force of my orgasm ripping through me. A swell of emotion unfurled within me, and I gasped, sweat forming on the back of my neck. As soon as I caught my breath and my vision cleared, I reached for Gabriel. Our mouths collided at this time, and I tasted my sweet juices on him.

He made a low growling noise and placed one arm on either side of me.

In the background, I heard Eric's sharp intake of breath. Gabriel pulled back after a while and looked over my shoulders. "What about now?"

The chair screeched as Eric stood up. "Bend her over and fuck her from behind."

Fire burned through me.

Before I knew what was happening, Gabriel had pulled me up to my feet. He placed both hands on my shoulders and kissed me so thoroughly that I was swaying by the end. Butterflies erupted in my stomach, and a thick fog of desire settled over me. Suddenly, Gabriel wrenched his lips away and spun me around. His hands moved over every inch of skin, leaving a trail of heat in his wake. When he pushed my breasts together, I moaned and leaned into his touch.

His fingers tugged and tweaked until my nipples were as hard as pebbles. When they were, he pushed my head forward. Wordlessly, I spread my legs apart and brought my elbows to rest against the back of the couch. I looked up, and Eric was in my line of vision. My lips lifted into a slow smile, mirroring Eric's, and he held my gaze as Gabriel thrust into me.

"Fuck." I breathed, my chest tightening. "You're so big."

"And you're so tight."

"Go slowly," Eric instructed in a strained voice. "Tease your way into her."

Gabriel eased out and pushed back into me. "You like that, don't you?"

I squeezed my eyes shut. "Fuck. You feel so good."

Gabriel ran a hand over my ass before giving it a light

slap. "That's it. I love your tight little pussy, and your big ass."

I released a deep breath. "Keep going."

Gabriel moved at a languid pace, as if we had all of the time in the world. My toes curled, and I ground against him, but he wouldn't indulge me. Instead, he dug his fingers into my hips and held me still. I whimpered and squirmed against him. He stilled, and I peeked over at Eric, who had a thin sheen of sweat on his forehead. Suddenly, Gabriel eased out and slammed back into me with a loud sucking noise.

I gripped the couch and moaned. "Oh, shit. Gabriel, you feel amazing."

Gabriel brought his head to rest against the back of my neck, and his pacing increased. We rocked back and forth against each other, our moans growing louder and louder, echoing back to us in the quiet apartment. Out of the corner of my eye, I saw Eric set down his drink and touch himself. His pupils dilated, and his mouth parted, and another rush of pleasure coursed through me.

"Fuck her harder," Eric said, in a strained voice. "That's it. Reach out and touch her."

Gabriel's hands darted in between my lips, and he pushed down, hard. I cried out and pushed down against him. "Oh, God. *Oh, yes.*"

Gabriel's tongue licked a path up my back. "You're so sexy, Lucy, and I love how you feel against me."

"I love how big you feel," I murmured, pausing to release a deep breath. "Keep fucking me, Gabriel. Don't stop."

Again and again, he slammed into me, skin slapping against skin. The smell of sweat and soap filled the air. When I couldn't take it any longer, I squeezed my eyes shut and rocked back and forth against him, reveling in the waves of pleasure that had built up within me. Gabriel's hands moved up and stopped on top of my breasts. He moved back and forth, tweaking my nipples with ease and speed.

Another wave washed over me, and I cried out.

Gabriel's pace slowed, and one hand stayed on my hips while the other moved over my back. I writhed and spasmed against him, a delicious rush exploding within me. When my vision cleared, I sucked in a huge breath and went still. My chest heaved, and sweat broke out across my back. Gabriel stopped, and we both looked at Eric, who had taken off his trousers. He was touching himself underneath his boxers, a strained expression on his face.

"Do you want to join us?"

Eric eyed Gabriel, and a slow smile spread on his lips. "Maybe in a bit."

Gabriel eased out and helped me to my feet. He laced his fingers through mine and pulled me towards the counter. In one quick move, he hoisted me up and settled in between my legs. I twisted my head to look at Eric and beckoned him forward. He stood up and pressed a kiss to my lips. I kissed him back, pouring as much emotion into the kiss as possible.

He made a low grunting noise in the back of his throat that sent a shiver of passion racing up and down my spine. I leaned forward and whimpered when Gabriel licked one nipple then the other. I wrenched my lips away and turned my attention to Gabriel, who had a strange glint in his eyes. He pressed a kiss to my lips, and his tongue darted out to lick my lips.

Eric wrapped a hand around the back of my neck. "Why don't we try something out? The three of us?"

I wrenched my lips away and smiled. "I'd love that. What do you think, Gabriel?"

Gabriel smirked. "I'm in."

CHAPTER 11

BIG FINISH

BY MARIE-CLAUDE

"Megan, I really don't think this is a good idea," I protested in a low voice. Pulsing music poured out of the speakers surrounding me, making the walls shake. I lowered my head and hurried after my sister, who was wearing a black dress that barely left anything to the imagination. On seven-inch heels, I wasn't even sure how she was able to walk, much less strut like she didn't have a care in the world.

When I caught up to Megan, she stopped in front of a pair of bodyguards and flashed them a smile. "We booked two private rooms."

One of the bodyguards eyed her intently. "Name?"

"Megan and Tia Barnes," she replied with a bored look.

In no time at all, we were being escorted to the back of the club, down a dimly lit hallway. We came to a stop in front of a set of black double doors that were pushed open. Inside, red and pink lights were dancing on the walls and giving the room a strange, eerie glow. As soon as the bodyguards left, Megan wheeled around and placed both hands on my shoulders.

"Babe, I say this because I care about you. You and Riley are in a rut, and I know you love him, but you need to spice up your sex life a little."

"By getting a lap dance? How is that going to solve anything?"

Megan straightened her back and winked at me. "What Riley doesn't know won't hurt him. You're not just getting a lap dance tonight."

"You didn't."

"I hired the male escort who helped Tim and me with our problems."

"You and Tim broke up," I pointed out, color rising up my cheeks. "This is crazy."

Megan patted my hand. "He's going to teach you how to dirty talk. Relax and enjoy."

With that, she tossed her blonde hair over her shoulders and walked over to the connecting door. She threw me one last wave and a kiss over her shoulder before the door clicked shut behind her. Once it did, I collapsed against the red leather booth and stretched my jean-clad legs in front of me. What is happening right now?

Suddenly, the door burst open, and a tall, well-built

Latin man walked in, with nothing but a black thong to cover his member.

I swallowed. "I don't think I'm supposed to be here."

He kicked the door shut with the back of my leg and walked over to me. "Relaxed. You've got nothing to worry about, *Bella*."

"My name is Tia."

Slowly, he lowered himself onto the booth next to me and smiled. "I know that isn't your name, but you are beautiful. I am Rafael."

I blushed. "Thank you, but I didn't know I was going to be—"

"Your sister explained everything," Rafael assured me. His eyes moved over my face and down the front of my shirt, stopping where it was tucked into my jeans. "So, you want to learn how to talk dirty while having sex with your husband."

I cleared my throat. "I never said that! But, yes... I want to spice up my sex life."

Rafael reached for my hand, and he pulled me to my feet. When he touched me, electricity raced through me, and I found myself yielding to him. Every inch of me came alive underneath his expert touch until I found myself standing in my bra and underwear. Rafael's tongue darted out to wet his lips.

"When you're dirty talking, you have to be as descriptive as possible," Rafael began. He knelt on the tile floor in front of me and tilted his head back. Slowly, he placed both hands on my ass and squeezed. "You are better than any fantasy I could ever come up with."

My heart hammered against my chest. "Thank you."

"Imagine I was your husband." Rafael's mouth moved over my bare skin, along the inside of my thighs. "What do you want me to do to you?"

I sighed. "I love your hands all over my body."

"Good. How does it make you feel?"

"It feels good."

Rafael brushed his mouth against my panties, his hot breath making shivers of delight race up and down my spine. "I love how you smell. I can't wait to taste you."

With that, he pushed my panties aside, and his tongue darted into my wet folds. My hands came up around his shoulders, and I gripped him hard. While I tried to think of Riley and how he'd feel if he was there, all I could think of was the gorgeous man between my legs, making me feel all sorts of things.

This is for Riley. Rafael is going to teach you how to dirty talk. Relax and enjoy the ride, Tia.

As soon as the thought crossed my mind, Rafael stopped licking and glanced up at me. "You taste so sweet. I could get Drunk off your juices."

My breath hitched in my throat. "I like how your mouth feels against me."

Rafael smiled. "Good. What else?"

My head spun when he ripped my underwear and tossed

it over his shoulders. Then, he pressed his mouth against me again, and gripped my hips. "I fucking love how your tongue feels inside of me."

Rafael made a low rumbling noise and continued to lick me.

My stomach tightened, and pressure built up inside of me. Wave after wave of desire rose in me until Rafael abruptly stopped and rose to his feet. Gently, he pushed me back, so I was sitting on the booth. With one hand, he pressed my breasts together and lowered his head in between them.

"Lift your arms up over your head."

Wordlessly, I did as I was told and held my breath. When he pulled a piece of rope out of his bag, I hesitated. But after taking a quick look at his face, I straightened my back and held still. Rafael tied both of my arms together. Then, he placed one leg on either side of me and thrust forward against my molten hot center.

"Tell me what you want," Rafael encouraged. "Remember, I'm your husband, and you're trying to drive me crazy. Men love a woman who can talk dirty and who knows what she wants."

"I want to feel you inside of me," I whispered after a brief hesitation. When I struggled against the binds, Rafael held them together. He circled his hips, making the figurative knots in my stomach tighten.

This was a bad idea, Tia. A really bad idea.

Except I couldn't bring myself to walk away.

Given that we were in a strip club, all I had to do was say the words, and Rafael would back off. Not only was this something he did for a living, but he also had to ensure customer satisfaction, or he wouldn't be able to make a living. Right? So, I opened my mouth to say something, but a whimper came out when Rafael placed his warm, calloused hands over my stomach.

"How do you want to feel me inside of you?"

"I want to feel you cum inside of me," I admitted, my ears turning hot. Rafael grunted and stood up. His eyes moved over me, searching for something. Suddenly, he removed his thong and sat back down, his tan and naked body glistening with sweat. Slowly, his hands touched my face and my shoulders before caressing down my back and coming to a rest against my ass.

I moaned when he rubbed himself against me. "There's nowhere else I'd rather be right now."

"Are you sure about that? What about if I was inside of you?"

I gasped when Rafael positioned himself at my entrance. "I love it when you're inside of me. All of you."

Rafael glanced up at my face and paused. "Do you want me to stop?"

I shook my head. "No."

Rafael thrust into me and released a deep breath. "God,

you're so fucking tight, and you sound so sexy. Tell me what you want me to do, Tia. Pretend I'm him."

"I want you fuck me," I choked out, the words ringing in my ears. Rafael moved against me, slowly at first and in long-practiced strokes. Eventually, his pacing increased until sweat formed on his forehead.

"Tell me more," Rafael urged in a strained voice.

"I love your dick inside of me." I threw my head back and moaned. Rafael's eased in and out, his heavy breathing reverberating inside of my head. In the background, I heard music wafting in from underneath the door, punctuated by the occasional giggle. Then, I squeezed my eyes shut and ground against him, earning a low growling noise in response.

What the hell are you doing, Tia? You're getting carried away.

Instead of stopping, I pushed the thought out of my head and focused on how Rafael felt inside of me, the smell of his Earthy musk washing over me. Desire built up within me, growing stronger and stronger until it ripped through me, and I gasped. By the time I caught my breath, Rafael had stopped moving and held completely still. He brushed my hair out of my eyes and pulled me to my feet.

Wordlessly, he bent me down and positioned himself behind me.

He gave my ass a smack and exhaled. "I wish I could control myself when I'm around you."

With that, he thrust into me, and my muscles expanded. I released a deep breath and tried to hear past the pounding in my ears. "Don't stop."

Rafael placed his head against my body, and his hot breath sent goosebumps up and down my arms. "Tonight is all about making you cry with pleasure."

I squeezed my eyes shut and ground against him.

We rocked back and forth, with Rafael easing in and out of me. A short while later, he shifted, placed one hand on either side of my ass, and gripped me, hard. Then, he began to pump me into me with an animal-like abandon, all while coaxing the deepest and darkest desires out of me. Until they were tumbling out of me in a rush.

"I want you to handcuff me and fuck me any way you like," I admitted, the butterflies in my stomach flapping mercilessly. "You bring out the animal in me. I love it."

"That's it, Tia," Rafael coaxed directly into my ear. He twisted my bound arms up over my back and tugged. "Tell me everything you want with as much detail as possible."

I loosed a deep breath. "This pussy is yours. Do with it whatever you want."

Rafael grunted, and his pacing changed, turning reckless again. "I want you to scream my name when you cum, Tia. How would you like that?"

"I would love that." I breathed. "Oh, God. Fuck me, harder."

Rafael grunted and growled until I came undone around

him. My entire body writhed and spasmed as I rode out my orgasm, gasping for breath the entire time. When my vision cleared, Rafael eased himself out of me and undid my binds. My hands fell limply to my sides, and I absent-mindedly began to rub them together.

Abruptly, I spun around to face Rafael, but he was facing away from me. "The key to talking dirty is not just about being honest about what you want but being open about what your man wants. Don't be afraid to try new things."

I swallowed. "Was that supposed to happen?"

"The best way to learn is to try. You're a natural, Tia, and your husband is going to love hearing you talk dirty."

"And if I need another lesson?"

Raphael smiled. "You know where to find me. And I have your sister's credit card on file."

CHAPTER 12
PAGING DOCTOR SEXY
BY KATE GOLD

Ray held up the white lab coat to the light and grimaced. "Really? This is what you want for your birthday?"

Jordan nodded and smiled. "You said we could do anything I want."

"I did, but I thought you were going to plan a trip to Disney World or something."

"We did that already."

"How about a movie marathon?"

Jordan shook her head and placed both hands on her hips. "No, I want to try on the costumes."

"We could watch porn instead," Ray suggested after a brief pause. He spun around to face her, a hopeful smile on his face. "Fine," he said with a laugh, "Anything you want."

"Ray, I know you don't want to admit because it's hard

for guys, but we're in a rut," Jordan reminded him. "This is one of the best ways to get out."

"We could do a threesome," Ray suggested, his face lighting up at the suggestion. "You, me, and a random hot woman."

Jordan chuckled. "Whoa, easy there, cowboy. Let's try roleplaying first and see where that takes us."

"I don't know if I can take it seriously."

"You're not supposed to." Jordan patted his hand and held up the lab coat to her body. "It's supposed to be fun and sexy."

Ray raised an eyebrow. "Okay, I guess we can try it out."

Jordan dropped the coat and drew Ray against her for a hug. "This is the best birthday gift ever."

"So, printing out a wish coupon wasn't such a bad idea?"

Jordan drew back and shook her head. "Not at all. I'm going to go change into my sexy nurse outfit and cash that coupon in."

"Or you could change in front of me," Ray suggested, with a quick wink. "I wouldn't say no that."

Jordan laughed and gave him a quick kiss. "I want it to feel organic."

Ray snorted. "We're about to carry out one of the most cliched forms of porn fantasy. There's nothing organic about this."

Jordan rolled her eyes. "Just go with me on this, okay?"

Ray held his hands up, eyes alight with mischief. "Alright, alright. I'll go put on my lab coat. Do you think I'm allowed to wear a shirt under this?"

"You can wear whatever you like underneath, although it's preferable if you don't wear anything at all."

Ray carried the coat in his arms and walked backward towards the guest room. "Don't spoil it for yourself, babe. Just have fun!"

Jordan grinned at the closet door.

Later, when she emerged in fishnet stockings and a lab coat that barely fell past her thighs, Jordan felt self-conscious. Especially when she caught a glimpse of herself in the full-length mirror and frowned at the scarlet red lipstick. With a shake of her head, she tossed her chestnut hair over her shoulder and stepped out of the bedroom. In the hall-way, she ran into Ray as he was doing up the last button.

His eyes widened when he caught sight of her. "Damn, you look hot."

Jordan cleared her throat. "I don't know what you're talking about, doctor Sexy—I mean Sexton."

"I like sexy better," Ray told her with a smirk. He paused and straightened his back. "When is our first patient coming in?"

Jordan checked her watch. "Not for a few hours, doctor."

Ray nodded and ran a hand over his face. "It can't hurt to prepare the exam room while we wait. Will you help me, Nurse?"

Jordan nodded and brushed past him, giving her hips a little extra sway. Ray reached for her on the way past, but she danced out of her reach. "Doctor Sexton, what's gotten into you?"

"It's Doctor Sexy," Ray corrected with a smile. He dove after her, but she jumped out of reach and stumbled out of the hallway. "You can't deny what's happening between us anymore, Nurse."

Jordan frowned. "I can. You're my boss, and I don't want to get in trouble."

Ray walked towards her, and she took a few steps back until she was pressed against the marble kitchen counter. "You're not going to get in trouble."

"We shouldn't," Jordan maintained, her voice catching towards the end. "What if we're caught? No one will ever hire me again."

"I'm not going to fire you," Ray assured her. He placed one arm on either side of her. "It'll be our little secret?"

Jordan batted her lashes at him. "Really?"

Ray nodded and placed a hand on the small of her back. "I wouldn't let anything happen to you, Nurse Titania."

Jordan's lips twitched. "It's Titania as in tight."

Ray leaned and brushed his lips against her ear. "I bet you are."

Jordan's breath caught in her throat. "I meant my name."

"I said what I said," Ray replied in a low voice. His hand moved from her waist to the front. He ducked underneath her coat and splayed his fingers over her stomach. Shivers raced up and down her spine. "Besides, I think Nurse Titania suits you a lot better."

Jordan blinked and tilted her head in his direction. "I don't know what you're talking about."

Ray's fingers moved up and caressed her breasts. "Yes, you do. Look at those tits."

"Someone is going to see, Doctor," Jordan protested, weakly.

"We don't have any patients coming in for hours," Ray said in a clearer voice. He leaned back and removed his hand. "We could have some fun in the meantime."

Jordan choked back a laugh. "What did you have in mind?"

Ray reached for her waist and pushed down her stockings. When they were around her knees, she stepped out of them and paused to kick them away. As soon as she righted herself, he pulled her to him, and his mouth covered hers. She sighed and grabbed a fistful of his coat. Then, she used her other hand to trace the length of his back and up to his neck. When she grabbed a fistful of his hair and tugged, Ray grunted into her mouth.

Holy shit.

Rather than wasting her wish coupon on another trip, she was glad she'd decided to switch things up. Not only was she enjoying the feel of Ray pressed against her in his pristine white lab coat, but she was getting the chance to act out one of her craziest fantasies. Years of Grey's Anatomy certainly hadn't helped.

"You're right, Nurse Titania. We shouldn't." Abruptly, Ray drew back and stepped out of her embrace.

Jordan covered the distance between them and tilted her head back to look up at him. "I changed my mind. We definitely should."

Ray shook his head. "No, we can't risk our jobs."

Jordan took a few steps back until her back collided with the counter. Her eyes stayed on his face as she hoisted herself up. Ray's eyes widened, but he said nothing, even as she spread her legs open, revealing the lacy black thong that left little to the imagination. Ray's entire expression changed into one of hunger, but he shoved his hands in his pockets and stayed still.

"Why don't you come over here and examine me, doctor Sexton?"

"It's Sexy," Ray reminded her in a low voice. She flicked a few buttons open and placed one elbow on either side of the counter. The lab coat rode up further, so her bare thighs were pressed against the counter. Ray made a low choking noise and covered the distance between them. Then, he tilted her head back and kissed her, so thoroughly that butterflies erupted in her stomach, and her toes curled.

When the need for air became too great, Ray ripped the

lab coat open and palmed her breasts. "I'm sorry about your coat, but it was getting in the way, and I need to do a thorough investigation."

Jordan smiled. "It's okay, doctor Sexy. I know you have to do what you have to do."

Ray's eyes moved over her face. His eyes stayed on her face as he reached behind her back and unhooked her bra. Her breasts spilled forward, and he immediately took a nipple between his mouth. He tugged and sucked before moving onto the other one, leaving both of them as hard rock-hard. Meanwhile, his hand moved between them before it ducked between her thighs and touched her over the fabric of the thong.

"Oh, doctor." Jordan breathed, tossing her head back. "That feels so good."

Ray pressed hot open mouth kisses over her chest and stopped when he reached her earlobes. "How does this feel?"

Jordan squeezed her eyes shut and moaned. "I know something that would feel better."

She shifted and reached for the hand between her thighs. Wordlessly, she placed Ray's hands on her pussy and ground against him. A second later, she heard a familiar ripping sound, and the blood in her veins turned molten. Then, Ray drew back, and a rush of cold air hit her center. She forced one eye open and saw Ray toss the lab coat onto the floor. His trousers and shirt followed soon after, leaving him in his boxers. He knelt down in between her legs and pressed his mouth to her. When he started to lick, Jordan arched her back and dug her nails into his shoulders.

Fucking hell.

His tongue darted out and licked a path upwards. Slowly, he moved back and forth, his hands braced on either side of the counter while she ground against him. Wave after wave of pleasure washed over her until she came. Her body writhed and spasmed on the counter while Ray held her still. When she was able to breathe again, Ray stood up and pulled down his boxers, revealing his erect member. She sat up straighter, spread her legs open, and beckoned him forward.

"You're so good to me, doctor," Jordan purred as he positioned himself at her entrance. When he thrust, she raked her fingers over his back and locked her legs over his ass. "God, your cock feels so good."

"It's a good thing we're doing this," Ray whispered into her ear. He gave a few quick thrusts, causing Jordan to whimper and moan. "You need me."

"I do?"

"Say it," Ray said, in a strained voice. "Tell me what you need."

"I need you to fuck me," Jordan told him, her eyes settling on his face. She held his gaze as he eased out and slammed back into her. A moan fell from her lips. "Oh, God. Doctor, you feel fucking amazing."

Ray buried his face in the crook of her neck and

continued to move against her. Back and forth, the two of them rocked against each other. Jordan squeezed her eyes shut, arched her back, and surrendered to the sensations, reveling in the waves rising with her. Every inch of her felt like it was on fire, and the only thing she could think of was how much more of him she wanted...needed. By the time another orgasm ripped through her, Jordan was covered in sweat and panting.

Wordlessly, Ray eased back and threw her legs up over his shoulders. Then, he thrust even deeper and made a low growling noise like a wild animal. The smell of his sweat and lemon-scented soap washed over her. Suddenly, he was thrusting at an increased and frenzied pace. It wasn't long before the two of them were moving against each other with wild and reckless abandon, hurtling closer and closer to the edge.

When Ray's mouth came up around her breast, she exploded yet again. White spots danced behind her eyelids and in her field of vision. She squeezed her eyes shut, gripping Ray, and riding out her orgasm. She sucked in a harsh breath and forced one eye open, then the other. Ray's head was still buried against her neck as he pumped in and out. Finally, he shot inside of her, shaking, warmth spilling between her legs.

As soon as he was done, he pressed a kiss on top of her head. "You'll need to come back for a follow-up, Nurse."

Jordan threw her head back and laughed. "Maybe on a bed next time?"

Ray gave her a devilish smile. "I think you mean the exam table."